Without Direction

Without Direction

Roy Johannesen

efp

the electric ferry press / kitchener

Published in Canada by The Electric Ferry Press

Library and Archives Canada
Cataloguing in Publication

Johannesen, Roy, 1942-
Without direction / by Roy Johannesen.

ISBN 978-0-9881098-0-3

I. Title.

PS3610.O23W58 2012   813'.6   C2012-904345-1

Cover image by Hannah Cook

For Gloria

1

With the arrival of spring to Southern Norway, Daniel Nordal woke early each day to walk before sunrise. In the predawn light, it seemed to him that he moved about in a smudged charcoal sketch. Sometimes, as he picked his way from cabin to cove, he thought he saw someone at the edge of his vision. Daniel Nordal did not believe in ghosts, but still, he was the only soul who lived on that island. Linda has returned from the sea, he thought once, but he pushed the idea from his mind as nonsense. Every morning he walked and watched.

When the sun restored the blue-green to the firs and the white to the birches, Daniel let the sea breeze dry his eyes, and then he returned to the cabin. On every even-numbered day, unless it was Sunday or a storm raged, he set out by boat at seven-fifteen for the mainland. On the last day that he followed that custom, he thought he heard a voice at the cove— Linda's voice.

When Lillesand harbour came into view, Daniel silenced the outboard and set the oars for rowing. He searched his pockets while the boat still had momentum, and pulled out his inhaler. With a self-conscious inhalation, he pulled the drug into his lungs. The boat started to roll—his second inhalation was quick. He dropped the inhaler in his pocket, wrapped his leathered palms around the oar handles, anchored his feet and pulled. When his chest felt lighter, he pulled harder.

At seven-fifty, Daniel shipped the oars, and let the boat slide alongside the dock. The shadow of the ore derrick fell exactly where it should if he were to reach Knudsen's at eight. Scanning the shore, he saw an old man rise from a bench, and he smiled. In Daniel's estimation, both the old man and the tide shared a desirable trait: predictability. Long ears held a watch cap high on the man's head so that Daniel thought he looked like an elf. Rolling up a thick layer of sweater from his wrist, the old man uncovered his watch.

"Is my timing off?" Daniel asked.

The old man shook his head and laughed. "I am just checking the accuracy of my watch." He chewed on an unlit pipe while Daniel unfolded himself from the skiff, and climbed onto the dock. "I admire a man who can row as you do, but I am curious. Why do you drag a motor behind the boat?"

Daniel heard this same question with each trip and so he created different answers according to his whim. "I have had only one piece of flatbread for breakfast. I weigh almost nothing now. So I need the weight of the motor to keep the boat trimmed." He could hear the old man laughing as he walked from the dock.

At eight o'clock, Greta Halversen unlocked the door to Knudsen's bakery just as Daniel stepped on the threshold. Without saying a word, Daniel went to the farthest table from the counter. He sat and stretched his legs; the opposite chair slid into the next table. With a mock scowl, Greta brought him a mug of black coffee and a plate with two raisin rolls.

A woman wearing a paint-stained canvas jacket bolted through the door and strode to the counter. "Hello Greta. Just coffee." Without turning her head, she said, "Good morning Daniel." The woman winked at Greta. "How do you get any work done with all his jabbering?" She laughed with Greta and brought her coffee to Daniel's table. His knees rammed the bottom of the table when the woman sat across from him.

"I thought you made coffee at the marina," Daniel said, and readjusted his chair.

"I need to talk with you. If you would get a mobile phone . . . oh never mind." Ingrid Larsen shook her head and sighed. "Well at least I know where to find you on even-numbered days. Why do you do that?"

Daniel stared at his coffee, and then he slowly raised his eyes to her. "Is it about the boat? Again?"

"No, but Daniel you should not use the motor—"

"I only row." He plucked the raisins from a roll and set them in a pile on the table. A chunk of roll plopped into his coffee.

"And I only fly." Ingrid stared at the flotsam in Daniel's mug and rolled her eyes. "You should not stress that boat by running the motor, but that is not why I came." She pulled her blond braid so it spilled over her right shoulder and played with its end. She leaned forward. "Someone has been asking for you at the marina."

"I have been expecting this. It is only natural that the king should want to consult with me. Would you like the raisins?"

"He only speaks English." Ingrid covered the raisin deposit with a napkin. "Why don't you order plain rolls?"

"Raisins give the rolls a nice flavour, but I don't care to eat them." Daniel scratched his bald crown. "It could be someone I met in America." He watched Ingrid play with the end of her braid.

She abruptly flung the braid back over her shoulder. "No, he does not know your name."

Daniel shrugged and fished a piece of roll from his mug, and then he jerked his head up. "Ha! Then how can he be looking for me? It is a salesman trolling for a bite."

Ingrid shook her head. "He said he was looking for the caretaker of the island that belongs to Ole and Anna Olsen. Listen to me Daniel. He is looking for you."

"He wants to sell something," Daniel said firmly.

"No Daniel. He said he is here to . . . make some changes on the island."

Daniel slammed his mug down and splashed coffee over

the table. "Anna would not do that to me . . . not without a word . . . a letter . . . something. And sending a . . . stranger." He looked into Ingrid's eyes. "Anna made a promise . . ."

Ingrid reached across the table and touched Daniel's hand. "This is probably nothing. Maybe a misunderstanding. Why not talk with him today, and clear this up?"

Daniel pulled his hand away. "Does this stranger have a name?"

Ingrid pulled a slip of paper from her jacket pocket and read, "Birk Olsen."

"Who is Birk Olsen? Is he related to Ole and Anna? They never mentioned him. What does he look like?"

"Puffy face." Ingrid puffed out her cheeks. "He looks a little like the lion man in the Wizard of Oz. But, a short lion man."

He uncovered the raisins and put one in his mouth. "Where can I find the lion man?"

"He said he would be at the Hotel Norge for a few days."

Daniel pushed the crumbs on the table into the raisin pile, and scooped everything into the half-full mug. "The coffee is terrible today." He counted out forty crowns and slapped the coins on the table. "I will see about this lion man." Daniel turned to the window and saw a cascade of water against the glass.

"Come to the marina after you see him," Ingrid said. "I will give you and that sad boat of yours a tow to the island."

"That is very considerate, but I can row all day in this weather."

Ingrid laughed. "I do not care if you row all week in the rain. I want to find out what this . . . Birk has to say."

Daniel stood in the lobby of the Hotel Norge, and cleared his throat. Water dripped from his sweater, while he waited for a sign that the clerk was alive. The clerk's eyes flickered in his direction, and then down to some papers on the counter. To Daniel, the glasses on the clerk's face appeared to be too small to be of practical value. Sliding down the man's nose, the glasses accelerated like a skier. When they jerked to a halt at the end of their tether, the man sighed and looked at Daniel. "Yes?"

"Ah, excuse me. I am looking for Mr. Olsen. Birk Olsen."

Shoving the glasses back on his nose, the clerk surveyed Daniel's clothes. "Who is enquiring?" The glasses came down the slope again.

Daniel felt his forehead tighten. "Who? Me of course."

"And you are?" The clerk cleared his throat. "What is your name?"

Daniel shrugged. "He would not know my name."

The clerk sighed. He lifted a handset to his ear and stabbed at a button. "I am sorry mister . . . there is no answer."

"Naturally, he must be having breakfast at this hour." He waited for the clerk to direct him to the dining area, but the clerk pressed the skier high on the slope and looked again at the papers on the counter. Stepping from the puddle at his feet, Daniel set out to explore the hotel. He had walked by this hotel hundreds of times, but had never been inside. His squishing feet carried him toward the interior, and as he walked, he heard the clerk cough and mumble.

The dining area was just behind the lobby where a few guests were eating, and from Ingrid's description, the lion man was easy to spot. Daniel watched Birk eat and observed that he passed over real food for corn flakes. Worse, he passed over coffee for tea. It would be hard to accept a man who eats corn flakes like a man feeding a furnace. He would not talk with a man who has a mouth full of cereal. He would wait.

The desk clerk came into the dining room, and glared at Daniel who now made a fresh puddle of rainwater near the buffet table. Daniel looked from the clerk to Birk and back again, and tried to decide which of these men made him more uncomfortable. With a grunt, he walked to Birk's table. "I think you are looking for me."

Birk glanced at Daniel, and brought another load to his mouth.

Daniel weighed whether he should walk away or demand respect, but then he remembered what Ingrid told him, and he spoke English. "I am Daniel Nordal."

Birk looked up and raised an eyebrow, but he continued to eat.

Daniel shifted his weight "I live on the island owned by Anna Olsen."

"Oh the caretaker." Birk spoke with a full mouth and sprayed cereal fragments over the table. "That's great Dan, now we can get to business."

Daniel leaned forward "Call me Daniel. I am not a care—"

"What do you call the island?"

"The island does not have a name, but you should know that. What do you want?"

Birk took another spoonful of corn flakes, and mumbled, "I suppose a boat comes with the property."

Daniel put his hands on the table. "Anna never mentioned you."

"I want you to take me to the island Dan."

"It is Daniel!" He jerked on the chair opposite Birk and dropped into the seat. "I do not work for you, and I know nothing about you."

"The island belongs to me, and I assume there must be a boat that goes with the property. I want you to take me to the island first thing in the morning." Birk pushed the cereal bowl away. "You can pick me up here." He glanced at the window. "Lousy weather."

Daniel felt as though he slipped on ice; he flailed and reached for a handhold. "What about Anna? Has something happened to her?"

Birk leaned back and folded his arms. "Anna Olsen is in a nursing home and can no longer manage her affairs." He picked up a pack of cigarettes and a disposable lighter from the table. "Tomorrow at eight-thirty then." Birk stood. "You know, I don't understand why the island should have a caretaker. I'll have to think that over. When we go to the island, you can tell me what it is you do there." Birk gave a curt nod, and walked to the lobby.

Daniel banged his fists on the table, and made the dishes rattle. He jerked to his feet, rushed through the lobby and slammed the entrance door.

At the harbour, Daniel saw his boat tied to the stern of Ingrid's sloop. When he came closer, Ingrid Larsen emerged on deck in foul weather gear, and waved Daniel aboard. He untied the bow and stern lines from their cleats and swung into the cockpit. "I will take the jib sheets," Daniel said without looking at her.

"When have I ever required extra hands to sail this boat? You are soaking wet—get below."

Daniel went forward and set loose the jib sheets. Ingrid opened her mouth to speak, but after looking carefully at Daniel's face, she took a position by the wheel. Neither of them spoke as they sailed to the island. Daniel adjusted and readjusted the jib as if the sloop were racing against a close competitor. Though rain-whipped, he never turned his face from the bow.

At the island, after securing the sloop and Daniel's boat, they sat across from each other at the table in the sloop's cabin.

Daniel looked past Ingrid and stared at the bulkhead, while she studied his face. After several minutes Daniel started to talk, and little by little, he told Ingrid what happened at the hotel.

Light filled the cabin as the rain ceased and the clouds dispersed. "I have bothered you enough Ingrid. It is time for me to go."

"What are you going to do?"

Daniel shrugged. "I have to think."

Ingrid put her hand on his. "You know I am your friend. Do you want to talk?"

Daniel shook his head and sat silently for a while. "I think I should visit the cove. Maybe an answer will come."

"Would it help if I came with you?"

He shrugged. "If you want to."

They climbed a muddy bank to a sod-roofed cabin, and then set out on a trail that followed the shore. "This trail circles the island," Daniel said. He paused to let Ingrid catch up.

"It is so worn. By you alone?"

"Yes, sometimes I walk for hours." He waited for Ingrid again. After five minutes they came to a cove.

The cove had a sandy basin ringed with boulders and clumps of birch trees. Sand extended into the water in a narrow band; otherwise, the shoreline was rocky. A bench, hewn from a single log, sat in an elevated position behind the sand.

Carved on the backrest, and highlighted with red paint was an inscription.

Linda og Emma Nordal
17 juli 1994

Daniel picked up a few twigs from the sand and tossed them from the cove. "It would be wild here in no time if I didn't keep up with it."

Ingrid came up beside him. "Do you come here every day?"

"Naturally, it is what I must do."

"Maybe if you explain, Birk would understand."

"No!" Daniel snapped his head around and looked intently at Ingrid. "I have known men like him; he would take advantage of . . ."

Ingrid sighed. "Forgive me Daniel, but maybe it is time to live your life again."

"What are you saying? How can you . . . a friend?"

"It is because I am your friend," she said softly.

"If I leave, or when I leave, will be my decision, and not this Birk telling me what to do. No, I cannot turn my back. Who is this man who thinks he can treat me like his servant?'

Ingrid put her hand on Daniel's arm. "You do not know him yet. Be patient. Just see what he has to say."

"You do not understand." He folded his arms and dislodged

Ingrid's hand. "I should refuse to bring him here." Daniel looked at the names on the bench, and then he turned toward the sea and sighed. After a few minutes, his face softened and he turned to Ingrid. "I am going to help Mr. Olsen make a decision. He will decide not to come here."

2

Before the sun rose, Daniel filled a soot-blackened pot with water and placed it on an alcohol burner. Then he counted, inspected, and placed thirty coffee beans into a hopper. He jerked the crank of the coffee mill in a circle; listened to the rumble of crumbling beans, and sniffed the hopper. When the water started to boil, he added the coffee. While waiting for the brew to gain strength, he looked at a photograph that hung on the cabin wall. A woman and a young girl stood smiling at the camera, and behind them was the cove. Daniel took the pot from the burner and tossed it into the sink. The flatbread and sardines that he had set out for breakfast—he threw into a trash pail. Then he set out along the shore trail. Colour had already come to the landscape. Daniel ran.

Short of breath and angry, Daniel sat on the bench at the cove. He tried to remember the good times with Linda and Emma, but his thoughts turned to the tragedy of the cove. He tried to lose himself in the ceaseless motion of the sea, but Birk Olsen dominated his mind. As the shadows grew short, all he could think about was the stranger, and anger blocked his tears. Daniel jumped to his feet; he was wasting time.

He tied up his boat at Lillesand Harbour, and was surprised to see the man with elfin ears sitting on his customary bench. It was an odd-numbered day, so he assumed that his experience would be different.

Daniel approached the man, and heard him ask, "Say captain, I see that you row, but why do you drag a motor behind you?" He felt unprepared; he was letting the old man down. All he could do was shrug.

The old man laughed and looked at his watch. "You are upsetting the rhythm of the harbour. This is the wrong day and the wrong hour."

You are right old man, Daniel thought. It is all so wrong. He saluted the old man, and then his thoughts turned to his task.

Birk was waiting for Daniel in the lobby of the Hotel Norge, wearing a thin yellow windbreaker that still had new-bought creases. Daniel guessed that Birk had made the purchase for the trip, and he noted with satisfaction that it would provide scarce protection in an open boat. The translucent material revealed a disposable camera and a packet of cigarettes. Daniel bowed slightly to Birk. "The boat is ready for you." Birk grunted and followed Daniel to the harbour.

Birk took two steps to every one of Daniel's at a pace that discouraged talking.

Without a word, Daniel lowered himself directly into the skiff and crawled to the middle seat. He studied Birk who was standing immobilized on the dock. He knew that Birk was too proud to ask for help. It would be as he expected. Daniel folded his arms and pretended to look away.

To Daniel's surprise, Birk came to the edge of the dock and turned his back to the boat. He wrapped his left foot and arm around one of the piles. Oh my God, he was going to slide down the pile, he realized, and suppressed his impulse to give warning. Birk manoeuvred his body so that he was hugging the post with his arms and legs. He started to slide, but his jacket caught on a nail head. As his body descended, his jacket bunched up under his arms. For a moment, the jacket stopped his descent. Daniel knew that Birk would break loose at any moment and fall in the water. A part of him wanted to see Birk wet, but no—he could not allow it. Perhaps Birk could not swim. Daniel jerked on the stern line to bring the boat closer to the dock, and Birk tumbled into the boat.

Birk hoisted himself into the stern seat, and sat there rubbing his knees. Maybe things were getting out of control. Birk could have been injured or even drowned—a terrible way to die. Daniel thought of Linda and Emma at the cove and shuddered. He surveyed Birk with his torn and grease-stained jacket and had doubts.

"The hell with you, and the hell with this boat," Birk said with a shaking voice.

Birk was safe, and there was nothing left but the plan. Daniel shrugged. "This is the only boat I have. The account I have is very modest, but you must know that. If you want to hire another boat, that is your choice."

Birk shifted his position on the bench and pulled the jacket tighter around him. "Let's get this over with," he said through clenched teeth. Birk glanced at a group of onlookers that had gathered on the dock. "Get the hell out of here!"

Daniel nodded and picked up the oars. As he turned the boat into the wind, spray flew to Birk as the oars blades came out of the water.

"Use the motor," Birk said.

"No, I cannot do that. Someone at the marina told me that the wood just behind you is too weak for the vibration. Naturally, I do not want to put you in danger."

Birk ducked as the oars came out of the water. "Then why the hell do you have a motor?"

Daniel thought about the answers he gave the old man on the dock and smiled. "Well, the clamps on the motor hold the stern together."

"Where's the island?" Birk tried to peer around Daniel.

"You cannot see it from here. After we leave the harbour, we will travel to the west. I will point it out when we get closer." The boat started to roll on the light chop.

Birk shivered, and attempted to wrap his jacket tighter. "Hold on there. How long is this trip?"

"Naturally that will depend on the current, the head wind, and so on. I think maybe an hour." He hoped it sounded believable.

"You're going to row the whole time?" Birk wiped water from his face.

"Of course."

"You're a crazy man!" Birk's arms started to flail about. "Turn this boat around. Now! I know what you're doing. Do you think I'm stupid?"

Yes Mr. Olsen, I would be happy to return you to Lillesand, Daniel thought. He pulled hard on the starboard oar.

Birk shook a finger at Daniel. "I'll hire a boat, and you're out of a job!"

Daniel stood on the dock and watched Birk limp away toward the hotel. Had he really accomplished anything? Then, he noticed the old man waving for him to come near. Daniel walked slowly in order to think of an answer to the expected question.

"The motor acts like a rudder. When I am rowing and there is a cross current, I turn the motor enough to create a balance. That way, I can pull with an even effort on both oars."

The old man clapped his hands, and took the unlit pipe

from his mouth. "The one time I was not going to ask, you give the best answer."

"Is there a different question today?"

"No question captain, just an observation. There are many places around the harbour where a passenger can easily board a small boat."

"Why do you call me captain?"

"You have the walk of a seaman. There is a heaving ship under your feet." He pointed to the bench with his pipe. "Sit down captain."

Daniel joined him on the bench. "There is no ship under me. One leg is shorter than the other. My name is Daniel Nordal. I watch over an island out there." Daniel waved his hand toward the sea. Then he extended his hand toward the man, who grasped it firmly.

"Eric Haugen, retired seaman. I worked with the NAL out of Oslo and Stavanger." He tapped the pipe against the bench. "You do not stay long in Lillesand when you come, so that explains it. You live on the island. Well, that is unusual. It must be a very important person you work for. In my experience, if anyone has their property watched in the skerries, it is just to have someone visit a few times off-season." Eric rubbed his chin. "Surely your unhappy passenger was not the owner?"

"Eric, how hard would it be for someone to find the location of an unnamed island?'

Eric raised an eyebrow. "If you know who owns it, it is

simple. Just look it up under the owner's name in the county office, and there you will find the location. Of course you would also need a nautical chart." He put the pipe in his pocket and looked intently at Daniel. "You do not want your passenger to find this island?"

Daniel sighed and nodded. "I believe that man is up to no good." As soon as he spoke, he had regrets. He just met this man—what was he saying? Could he trust him?

"Of course this matter is none of my business," Eric said. "If you will allow a suggestion?" Daniel nodded. "If this person is up to mischief, do you not want to know about it?"

"I do not understand."

"Well, you want to know what he is doing. Do you not? If he finds the island without you . . ."

Daniel considered what Eric told him; it seemed to make sense, but he wondered why this man would take an interest. "I will not get him to step into that boat again. Maybe I did not plan very well." A headache was boring into his forehead, and he knew he must have coffee. Daniel started to rise, but the old man grabbed his sleeve.

"I think I can help you captain."

Relieved to find a new face behind the hotel's front desk, Daniel inquired about Birk Olsen. After a brief telephone exchange, the woman directed him to room 203.

Birk began to shout as soon as he unlocked the door. "Why

can't I get any help in this country? Tell me what is going on here? What's out there that you don't want me to see?" He pointed toward the window. "The water taxi never heard of Olsen's island. Did you talk to them? And look at this" He grabbed his torn jacket from a chair and pressed it close to Daniel's face. "It's ruined because of your game."

Daniel looked at the wall behind Birk. "I forget myself sometimes, and I think everybody is comfortable around boats. Of course it is my fault. But, I think I have a solution to your problem." Daniel closed the door to the room.

"You have nerve. Make it quick."

"I can arrange for a forty-foot motor launch with a cabin to take you to the island. You can hire it for a fair price."

Birk cocked his head to one side and squinted. "And you will tell the skipper where the island is?"

"No, I will show the captain where the island is."

"Oh no, I don't trust you. I'm not going to sea with you and a stranger."

"Very well. I will give instructions to the captain and I will be on the island when you arrive."

"No, you will be off the island."

"There will be no boat then." Daniel reached for the door. "You are a stranger making claims. I have to be cautious. Naturally, I will have to see legal papers and so on. Until then, the island is my responsibility. So you see—you cannot dismiss me. As far as I know the owner is still Anna Olsen, and I know I have her support. So, Mr. Olsen, if you want to see the island, you should look for a forty-foot wooden launch on the west side of the harbour. It will be near the derrick. The captain is Eric Haugen, and he will expect you at nine tomorrow morning." He opened the door. "The captain will not wait." Daniel strode from the room, and his focus returned to the pain in his head.

The dub-dub-dub of a slow-revving diesel brought Daniel from his cabin to the dock. He saw two figures in the wheelhouse, and it occurred to him that he had not given the visit sufficient thought. Maybe this was all a bad idea. Nevertheless, there they were, and he would have to deal with it. He could let Birk struggle for every bit of information, but then he may not learn what he needed. He would humour Birk and see what happens.

Eric set out a ramp, and Birk strode straight and stiff across it to the dock. Daniel thought he looked like a child pretending to be King Harold. The illusion was broken when Birk pulled a pack of cigarettes and a disposable lighter from his pocket. When the lighter failed, he threw it to the ground, and mashed the cigarettes in his fist. Frowning, he pointed a finger at Daniel. "Let's start with the buildings." He waved for Eric to follow.

Daniel led the party up to the top of a bluff where they entered the cabin. The room they entered contained a compact kitchen, a table with one bench and two chairs, a sofa that could double as a bed, and a wood burning stove.

"Very nice woodwork," Eric said. "Who did this?"

"I do not know who built the cabin," Daniel said, "but I did most of the finish work you see. I am a carpenter by trade."

Birk pushed open a door and discovered a bedroom with two built-in bunks. "I have a closet bigger than this. No bathroom?"

"There is a latrine outside, in the back of the cabin. And I have an outdoor shower."

Birk rolled his eyes. "What about water?"

"Rainwater is collected in a cistern. There is a storage tank under the sink."

Birk slammed the bedroom door. "Show me the other buildings."

Daniel considered this latest command. There never were other buildings, and Birk should have known that. Was he a fraud or a fool? He decided to probe. "Ah Mr. Olsen, did you want to see the main house next?"

Birk's eyes widened. "Of course I do." He looked around the cabin and shook his head. "My father liked to live well. Not like this."

"Your father?" Daniel shook his head. "No, Ole liked to get back to simple things when he came home to Norway. This is where he lived. It is the only building on the island. You never heard this from your father?" How odd, that Ole never talked about having a son. And how can a son not know about his father?

"I don't believe my father would live here. Show me the rest of the island."

Daniel shrugged and led the two men along the shore trail. When they came to the cove, Birk wanted to stop and explore.

"This has promise," Birk said. "Clear out those boulders, level that rise, and there is room for development." He pointed to the shore. "A load of sand will make that a beach. A beach is a good selling point."

Daniel grabbed his arm. "What are you talking about?"

"Let go of my arm. I'm talking about summer cottages."

"There are strict laws about development. No, you cannot do that in the skerries." Daniel released his arm. "And there is no water here."

Birk laughed. "All you ever need is a good lawyer, and money in the right hands. I would never have survived on Long Island if I worried about regulations. Sometimes, it's best just to go ahead and take care of details later."

"This is not Long Island." Daniel started to tremble. "The current here is dangerous. A swimming beach is out of the question."

"That's my business. A beach sells property, and my job is to sell—"

Daniel reached out, grabbed Birk by the shoulders, and

spun him so that they were face to face. "You do not seem to hear me. I am talking English to you. The water is very deep. Two people drowned here." He started to shake Birk. "My daughter could not fight the current." Daniel choked. "She drowned! My wife tried to save her." He grabbed Birk by the collar. "She drowned! Do you hear me Birk?"

"Stop," Eric said in Norwegian, "If he tries what he says, you only have to report him to the county officials. Let him go. You are only making trouble for yourself."

"I do not trust him Eric. What am I going to do?" He released his hold, and Birk backed away. Daniel pressed close to Birk again. "Have you talked about developing this island with Anna Olsen?"

"I don't need to discuss anything with my stepmother."

"I see. The tour is over Mr. Olsen. For now, the island is my responsibility. The law in Norway says anyone can walk here." Daniel leaned down and placed his face close to Birk's. "But nobody can disturb land that is not theirs."

"Just a minute, this land is—"

"Nobody!" Daniel pointed to the trail. "The boat is that way."

After Eric and Birk left the cove, Daniel pulled his inhaler from his pocket, and used it over, and over, and over. Then he scrunched down on the sand, and tasted the saltwater that ran down his face.

3

Daniel woke to the sound of snapping twigs, so he pushed himself up on his elbows. The shadow of a birch had rotated more than a quarter turn since Birk and Eric left him. Perhaps he imagined the noise, or maybe it was a fragment from an unremembered dream. Then the noise became obvious, and it was close. He looked toward the trail and when he saw Eric, he forced his aching body to stand. Where was Birk?

As if he could read Daniel's mind, Eric said, "I am alone. Do you mind if I join you?" Not waiting for an answer, Eric came to where Daniel stood. "Are you okay?"

Daniel wiped drool from his cheek. "I just woke up. Come to the bench." Daniel trudged to the head of the cove, and slumped on the bench where Eric joined him.

"When I took Mr. Olsen back to Lillesand, I thought of how disturbed you looked. It did not seem right to leave you alone," Eric said.

"Being alone is best. There was no need."

"There is no sense in that. Being alone is never best." Eric pulled a bottle of cherry brandy from his coat and thrust it toward Daniel. "I was saving this for my next cold, but winter is over. Perhaps, you can use some now."

Daniel stared at the bottle but did not touch it. *What should I think of Eric? He said he came here out of concern, but still he mocks. How could Eric possibly understand?* Daniel shook his head and Eric withdrew the bottle.

"Would you like me to leave?"

What is happening to me? Now I am being rude. "No, you have come a long way. Thank you. Perhaps just a sip."

They sat quietly for many minutes, passing the bottle back and forth. *What was the fuss about? Eric was trying to be helpful.* "That was very kind of you to return." Daniel felt his face grow warm. "You should finish this." He lifted the bottle in the air.

Eric shook his head. "I still have to pilot a boat this evening." He hesitated. "That must have been a terrible thing for you . . . What happened here?"

Daniel sighed. "Look behind us—up there on the ridge is a rocky ledge. I climbed up there because of the excellent view of the skerries. It was a warm day and my mind was drifting, and then I heard a scream. When I looked toward the cove I saw Linda running into the sea." Daniel took a deep breath. "Emma was beating at the water, and her head was going under. She was a good swimmer, but the current was too strong. I could see that Linda was going to help her." He took another sip of brandy. "I tore straight down—through the brush—as fast as I could. When I came here . . . there was no one in sight. Naturally, I rushed into the water and I swam and I dove again and again." He turned his face from Eric. "I should have stayed Eric. I should have stayed out there until I found them or drowned." Daniel's shoulders heaved. "They are here; I cannot leave them alone."

"What a dreadful burden you bear. I can understand how you must feel about this place. Here, finish the brandy."

Daniel tipped the bottle to his mouth, wiped his chin with his hand, and turned to Eric. "Anna, Birk's stepmother, told me the island was to remain as it is, but I could stay here as long as I wished. When she dies, ownership goes to the county." He emptied the bottle.

"How do you know this woman?"

"I went to America just out of school, where I lived with my uncle and became a carpenter's apprentice. I met Linda, and in time we married and then Emma came into our lives. We bought a house on Long Island, and we came to know the Olsen family. Do you know they came from Lillesand? Well, they had this island property that they used in the summer. As they grew older, they came here less often. We had an open invitation to vacation here, and in return I did some work on the cabin."

"It is getting chilly. Come to the cabin for coffee," Daniel said. They started to walk. "After Ole Olsen died, Anna became ill, and so we were the only ones to come here. It was so wonderful to come here, but then . . ." Daniel cleared his throat. "So, I went home and sold everything. I had to come back here, to be close. Anna told me to stay as long as I needed. She even set up a small fund at the bank for repairs and taxes and so on." Daniel threw his hands up. "I never heard of Birk until now."

In the cabin, they drank coffee together, and the talk turned to boating, the weather, and taxes. At dusk, Eric departed, and Daniel slumped on the sofa and fell into a deep sleep.

Daniel woke at one in the morning with a headache. While he fumbled with a lantern, he thought about Eric. Because Birk hired him, would Eric feel duty-bound to do Birk's bidding? Daniel opened a bag of coffee beans. Eric never offered an opinion about Birk. He counted thirty beans. Was the brandy to get him talking? He scooped up the beans and threw them in the hopper. He talked too much. Daniel felt his arm spinning faster and faster, and realized the beans were already ground. With a grunt, he tossed the ground coffee in the trash pail. He stared at his reflection in the window, and decided to visit the county offices that morning.

To avoid Eric, Daniel brought his boat to the marina on the east side of the harbour. Perhaps Ingrid can give me an opinion, Daniel thought. When he found her, she was working with a shipowner to adjust the tension on the mast shrouds of a schooner. Not wanting to disturb her, he set out alone along the harbour until he came to Østregata, and entered the county offices at number two. A clerk, who reminded him of St. Nicholas, provided him with the property record for the island. The property was registered to Ole and Sigrid Olsen in 1965. *Sigrid?*

Daniel asked the clerk about the effect of a divorce and re-marriage on property rights. The clerk reached to his face, and seemed to be searching in his beard for an answer. "That is a legal matter. It varies, depending . . ." He reached for the paper and studied it. "See here." He turned the paper around so Daniel could see where his finger pointed. "Right here. The record was amended so that Sigrid was deleted and Anna was added."

Daniel felt the band around his head relax. "What happens when the owners die? Is there a will?"

"That would not be kept by the county."

Daniel drummed his fingers on the counter. "Can property change hands without your knowledge?"

The man shook his head. "When property ownership is transferred for any reason, it must be recorded here."

Daniel still had time to act. He thanked the man and walked from the building in a daze. He took the longest possible route around Lillesand Church to the marina, and saw Ingrid sitting on the seawall by his boat. "Are you waiting for it to sink?"

"I was wondering," Ingrid said, "why do I smell gasoline around your boat when you say that you never use the motor?"

"Naturally, it smells of gasoline. It has a gasoline motor."

"Do not tempt fate." She looked closely at Daniel's face, and raised an eyebrow. "You look worn out. Are you okay?" She listened quietly while Daniel explained what had happened with Eric and Birk. "You made Birk your enemy from the start. Maybe he would have a different attitude if you were civil to him."

Daniel dug his fingers into his knees. "You have not met the man. How can you take sides?"

Ingrid sighed. "I wish you could see that I am on your side, but I see you have made up your mind. Oh, the reason I waited for you. I have some good news. Solveig Jacobsen will be here tomorrow."

Daniel shook his head. "It is not a good time."

"Daniel, it is never a good time for you, but you need to do something different. It will be a good change, and it will be nice to see her again. We will meet her at the Kettle dining room after I finish work. Meet me here, and we can go together."

Daniel moaned. "This could not have happened at a worse time."

When Ingrid finished work the following day, Daniel was

waiting by her Volvo. Her eyes widened, and she smiled when she saw him. "You came! Look at you. And a sweater without stains."

"I came for a good meal."

Ingrid winked. "Of course you did."

Daniel shook his finger at her. "And what a price I will have to pay."

Ingrid laughed and they climbed into her car. On the drive to The Kettle, Daniel wanted to talk about Birk and the island, but Ingrid refused to discuss the topic.

Solveig Jacobsen was waiting in the lobby when they arrived. Her dress was better suited for the Oslo opera than the casual Kettle dining room. Solveig was a hugger, so Daniel tried to avoid the perfumed crush by pretending to accept her hand when she reached for him. His attempt was not even a speed bump for Solveig. She engulfed him without mercy.

"Yes, it is good to see you both," Solveig said. Daniel winced. She said her "yes" with a peculiar intake of air. It was as if she must fill her lungs as rapidly as possible while saying it. They selected a table, and the women sat across from each other. Daniel sat next to Ingrid. Their decision was unanimous; salmon fillets with boiled potatoes and sliced cucumbers.

While they waited for their meals, Solveig brought them up to date on her business. Her tourist shops in Oslo and Bergen were turning a good profit. In the past year, she opened a new summer shop in Geiranger. Her shops sold sweaters, silver jewellery, woodcarvings, and a host of souvenirs of Norway. She believed that summer shops were the best way to expand her business, and she was on her way to Lyngør to look at some property. "The village of Lyngør is spread over four islands you know." She directed her gaze at Daniel. "You live on an island. I do not believe I have ever been there."

"Only one inhabitant, a summer shop would not survive," Daniel said.

The women laughed. "With plans for development," Ingrid said, "maybe a shop will do well."

"What's this?" Solveig asked.

Ingrid turned to Daniel. "I should not have said anything."

"A problem Daniel?" Solveig asked.

"Nothing—" Ingrid started.

"Maybe I should explain for Solveig." Daniel described his meetings with Birk.

"If he is a contractor he must have a reputation. Maybe we can learn something. I have many contacts in America. I once worked for an importer in New York, you know. Perhaps I can dig up something about this Birk Olsen."

Daniel held up his hands. "No, no, this is my problem."

"Yes, I insist. For old times sake."

While they dined, their conversation shifted to food and restaurants. When they finished and the coffee was served, Ingrid asked Solveig how long she would be in Lillesand.

"I must travel to Arendal tonight. You see, I did not plan very well. Both the Hotel Norge and The Kettle have a full house, and it will be too late to get a ferry to Lyngør." Solveig looked at her watch. "Yes, I had better leave now."

"No, no, we can put you up," Daniel said. He expected that Ingrid would jump in and offer to share her apartment as she had in the past.

"What a good idea," Ingrid said. "Daniel has an extra room. You wanted to see the island where Daniel lives, so this will be a fine opportunity. You can ride with me in the sloop." Daniel leaned hard against Ingrid, and he felt her body shake with contained laughter.

Daylight was fading as the sloop, with Daniel's boat in tow, arrived at the island. Solveig had more suitcases for an overnight stay, Daniel decided, than he would require for an Arctic expedition. He took a covert puff from his inhaler and proceeded to shuttle the load up to the cabin.

At his first opportunity, he hissed in Ingrid's ear. "You seem unusually happy this evening."

She pulled back. "Do not spit in my ear. It is about time you entertained."

"I cannot row her to the harbour in the morning with all her ballast. Will you stay too?"

Ingrid grinned. "Oh, I would love to, but it is my turn to make coffee tomorrow morning at the marina."

"Come back in the morning as soon as you can," Daniel said through clenched teeth. "Shhh, Solveig will hear you."

Eventually, Daniel moved Solveig's luggage, and Ingrid sailed to Lillesand. Then Daniel had to face the dilemma of a woman spending the night in the cabin. He moved her things into the bedroom and set up the sofa for himself.

"This is so kind of you to let me stay here. The cabin is so cute. It reminds me of the mountain cabin my father had for skiing." A frown crept over her face as she looked around. "So Daniel, where can I freshen up?"

"Of course, just behind the cabin. Here, there is an extra lantern for you." He gave her directions and a basin of water that he filled from a pump at the sink.

"Thank you, I think I can manage." Furrows appeared on her forehead.

An hour went by while Solveig shuttled between the bedroom and darkness. After much snapping of luggage latches, Solveig emerged from the bedroom and sat at the table. Daniel offered coffee, which Solveig declined.

"Come sit down Daniel, I have not talked with you in a long time."

Daniel sat across from her, and searched his head for topics of conversation. All he found was a headache.

"Do I make you uncomfortable?" Solveig asked.

"No, of course not." Daniel's head throbbed.

"The woodwork here is so fine. Even out back. Do you know who did it?"

"The cabin was run down when the Olsens bought it. I did some work for them"

Solveig leaned toward him. "You? How wonderful! I need a carpenter from time to time, and I will certainly need one if I buy the property in Lyngør. Would you be willing? I am willing to pay well for such quality work."

"No, I cannot leave. It is out of the question, but thank you for the offer."

Solveig pouted. "Surely you are not bound to stay here forever?"

"I am bound for now." He rubbed his temples. "I think I will have some coffee. Is there anything I can get for you?"

Solveig declined, and while Daniel prepared coffee, she talked about their school days in Lillesand. "When you finished school and your family left for America, it broke Ingrid's heart."

Daniel shook his head. "She was just a child. Maybe eleven years old."

"Eleven year old girls have crushes you know. You were a very sophisticated teenager to her."

Daniel forced a laugh. "We were both just children."

"She told me that she wrote to you in America, but you never replied."

"I do not remember."

Solveig looked around the room. "Living like this—do you get lonely?" Daniel shook his head. "I guess you would not. I remember that you always seemed . . . I do not know how to put it . . . to keep your distance."

Daniel stood at the sink and spoke to Solveig's reflection in the window. "I remember an old saying: 'He who walks alone, walks best'"

"Forgive me Daniel, but where did you hear such nonsense."

4

After a sleepless night, Daniel watched the morning light spread a rippled shadow along the wall of logs. Suddenly, Solveig emerged from the bedroom. She stretched, smiled, and wished Daniel a good morning.

"I have not slept so well in years," Solveig said. "It is so peaceful Daniel. Now I understand why you like it here. Maybe this is what I need—an island cabin." She sighed. "But still, it would be too lonely." She walked to the door, swung it open, and gulped deep breaths.

It occurred to Daniel that he was responsible for providing breakfast. He did a mental inventory of his larder, and realized that he was in trouble. "Perhaps you would like to stroll about while I prepare breakfast."

He set about to boil coffee. There was a box of pancake mix that required only water, and a jar of cloudberry preserves. A tin of herring would round out the meal. The pancake mix had passed its expiration date by a year, but it looked okay and did not smell. Heat from the griddle would destroy any vermin. There was no shortening, but a residue in the pan caused everything to slide. When breakfast was ready, he went to the door and called. He braced himself. A big-breath "yes" was certain.

"Yes, this reminds me of when I went camping as a little girl."

Daniel had trouble picturing Solveig as a camper, and the image of her as a little girl was fuzzy. He guessed he would survive the morning, but how would he get her luggage to Lillesand?

"I could smell the coffee all the way to the dock. It must be good and . . . hearty. Maybe just some water for me." Her smile appeared strained as she sat and cut the pancakes. She pushed the pieces around her plate and stacked them to make pancake islands. "The cloudberry preserves are delicious."

The crack of a sail spilling wind filled the air. Just what I need, Daniel thought. Ingrid will expect breakfast. Will this morning never end, and let peace return? He considered opening a tin of mackerel.

After several minutes, Ingrid arrived carrying a basket filled with rolls, brown goat cheese, waffles, a jar of lingonberry preserves, oranges, apples, and a vacuum bottle of coffee. As soon as she placed the food on the table, Solveig stacked her pancake segments into a pile that seemed to reduce their bulk. Ingrid announced that she had already eaten, so she stood by the table and encouraged Solveig and Daniel to enjoy the food. Solveig needed no encouragement, but Daniel resolved to eat only what he had prepared.

He weakened as he worked on the chewy pancakes, so he slid his food aside, and palmed a roll. At the edge of his vision, he saw Solveig watch him take the food, and she turned to Ingrid and winked. Daniel put the roll down on the table and ate no more.

More than anything, Daniel wanted to walk, but he felt obliged to remain with his visitors. His mind wandered the island trail, but a part of his consciousness heard Ingrid and Solveig chatting. The talking reminded him of droning bees and he decided that the sound was soothing.

Solveig talked about a man named Tom.

There was work to do at the cove, Daniel realized. Debris would have washed ashore since his last visit, and it would require his attention.

She met Tom in Oslo.

He could even walk around the island—maybe twice. The women would never notice his absence.

Tom had a daughter, Solveig was saying.

He would pretend to take the coffee grounds outside, and then he could disappear.

The dub-dub-dub of an engine focused his mind. Daniel went outside and climbed on a rock for a clear view of the dock. He recognized Eric's launch at once. Birk debarked, followed by a woman and a child. The woman appeared to be much younger than Birk; she was taller as well. She was assisting a boy, who Daniel guessed was about five years of age.

Eric stayed with the boat while his three passengers picked their way up the trail to the cabin. Daniel rushed into the room. "Birk is coming up the trail, and he has a woman and a child with him."

"It is very complicated Ingrid," Solveig said. "If it was just Tom, I would not have a problem."

"I said Birk is coming this way."

"Does his daughter accept you?" Ingrid asked.

"May I interrupt you two? We have company."

"Just a second, Daniel," Ingrid said without looking at him.

Solveig shrugged. "She is a quiet girl, and it is hard to know what she thinks."

Daniel started to speak, but Ingrid held up her hand. "She is probably not used to you. Why not plan an outing for the two of you?" She turned to Daniel. "Try being patient with Mr. Olsen; let us see what happens. Please?"

"An outing is a good suggestion," Solveig said. "I am still a stranger to her."

"You really do not understand the situation," Daniel said.

"Yes, now we have company." Solveig started to pick up the plates from the table.

"I should tell them to go away." Daniel started for the door, but Ingrid grabbed his arm.

"You are so stubborn Daniel. Listen for a change." Ingrid turned to Solveig. "How old is Tom's daughter?"

"Birk does not speak Norwegian," Daniel mumbled.

"Ten, and her name is Sarah."

The muffled sound of voices came through the open window. "Company is here," said Ingrid. She pushed past Daniel and opened the door. "Hello, I am Ingrid Larsen," She said in English. A chain of introductions followed, but Daniel remained mute. The woman was Laura, Birk's wife, and the boy was Robert, the couple's son.

"I'm going to take another look at the cove," Birk said.

"You go ahead," Laura said. "Robert is too tired for walking. I'll wait here for you." She slumped on the sofa, and lifted the boy onto her lap. Laura looked in turn to Ingrid, Solveig, and Daniel. "I hope you don't mind if I rest here." Robert squirmed on her lap. "I'm in Norway for a brief stay, and I just had to see the project Birk was so excited about."

Daniel slipped out of the cabin and followed Birk, but his footfalls were sufficiently loud to cause Birk to stop and turn. "So, I see you're not a hermit after all," Birk said. Daniel just stared at him with his arms folded. "Look Dan . . . ah, Daniel. I can see you have a problem with this business, but it's nothing personal. If you want to help me, I'll overlook what you said before. Otherwise, it would be best for everyone if you packed up and got out of here. There's work for you clearing the cove if you want it."

"Daniel!" Ingrid called from the cabin. "Daniel we need you here." Daniel felt his muscles tighten and he stepped closer to Birk. His vision blurred. He saw a face close to his, and a mouth that opened and closed. Then he saw a man rushing away. His body trembled, and he was unsure what was happening to him. A hand touched his arm gently. Ingrid was at his side.

"Where is Birk?" Daniel asked.

Ingrid shook her head. "He went away. Come inside," she said softly.

"This is a dream come true for Birk," Laura was saying. When Robert saw Daniel, he buried his face in Laura's arm. "I hope he keeps the cabin. It's so lovely here." She turned her attention to Daniel. "I can see why you love it here. Anna was very fortunate to find a caretaker like you. I'm sure Birk will compensate you for all your work."

Daniel glanced at the picture of Linda and Emma. "I am not a hired caretaker."

Laura frowned. "I'm sorry, I thought—"

"Would you like some coffee? Perhaps a waffle?" Ingrid asked. Laura declined.

Daniel collapsed onto a wooden bench. "Has Anna signed over the property to your husband?" He heard Ingrid sigh.

"Oh, it's too complicated for me. Birk doesn't think Anna needs to sign anything, but I don't know. He's working with a lawyer, but everything takes time," Laura said. Daniel leaned forward, and Ingrid stepped in front of him.

"How old is your boy?" Solveig asked.

"He just turned five." Her face brightened. "Oh, he will love it here. Birk said there is a lovely little beach."

Daniel stood and opened his mouth, and Ingrid gave him a look he had never seen on her face before. He cleared his throat and approached the sofa.

"There is something you should know," Daniel said, his voice shaking.

"Laura," Birk called from outside. "It's time to go. Now!"

In a fog, Daniel watched the family walk down the trail to Eric's launch. Ingrid said she had to get Solveig back to the mainland. In a haze, he watched as everyone left until at last, silence descended, and he could walk again.

"Oh, he will love it here. Birk said there is a lovely little beach." Laura's words played over and over in Daniel's mind. It was all he could think of the rest of the day and into the night.

He dreamed of Robert screaming, and struggling in the water, and he woke the next morning drenched in sweat. There was no question in Daniel's mind; the cove was dangerous and he had to stop Birk. The sea would not claim another life as long as he could stop it. Birk was unreasonable, so he would have to talk with Laura. What mother would knowingly endanger her child? She was here for a short visit, so he must work quickly. His decision to act calmed his mind, and he fell into a deep sleep and woke well after sunrise.

Daniel skipped breakfast and his morning walk, and set out at once for Lillesand. The outboard will run at full throttle for the entire trip, he decided. It no longer mattered what anyone would think, or even if the boat were damaged; he was saving the life of a child. An innocent child like Emma.

After motoring for ten minutes, he saw water pooling under his feet. There were no obvious leaks. It must be spray. The water line rose, but not enough to threaten the boat. His mission was too important to let a little water deter him. To be safe, he decided to remove his boots and use his socks to sop up at least some of the water. With his right hand on the throttle, he used the left hand to dip his wadded socks in the water at his feet, then to reach over the gunwale and squeeze the water out.

His chest felt heavy, and he realized that he had not used his inhaler that morning. The excitement of his mission, and the constant bending, added to his distress. Daniel searched in one pocket after another; then searched the same pockets again. Then panic amplified his distress. Soon he was breathing as through a straw, and he could no longer bend. Lillesand harbour was closer than the island, so he decided to continue.

His feet were cold and wet, and the wind in his face seemed to suck any remaining air from his lungs. The work of breathing became his focus. It was unbearable to sit on the bench, but standing was impossible. He wanted to give himself to the sea, and end his suffering, but he remembered Robert. Should he go to the clinic or the hotel first? The hotel was closer, and more important—Laura was there. Sometimes strong coffee helped. There would be coffee at the hotel. First he heard buzzing in his ears, and then the sound of the engine faded away.

The harbour? So soon? Did I sleep? He discovered that he was leaning forward, his weight supported by his grip on the throttle. All of his muscles complained. His chest hurt the most. A chest of cement.

He would never be able to climb onto a dock, he realized. *The beach closest to the hotel! Yes, there are no bathers this time of year.* He set a course for the beach, and as he approached, he cut speed to where he guessed he would have enough way to slide on the sand. The boat stopped abruptly on the beach, but Daniel kept his grip and remained on the bench. He had to use his left hand to pry his right hand from the throttle. Daniel rolled over the gunwale onto the sand, and struggled to his feet.

A shout caught his attention, and he saw Eric running. Daniel tried to wave him away, but he had no energy. He turned his concentration to putting one foot in front of the other. *There is no air. How can I do it? Just move.* After a few steps, he stopped and leaned forward onto his thighs. With all his strength, he pulled an insignificant amount of air into his lungs, and took another step.

Eric shouted—a call for help. Daniel could not speak; he just shook his head and tried another step. Eric took his arm, and Daniel willed himself, without success, to be free. Daniel's thoughts drifted to other days, and other places. And the noises of the harbour died. It was a strange dream. The world moved in slow motion. The roar of an engine disturbed him. Shouts! Close? Far Away? Many hands were upon him. Hands lifted him from the beach. He fought the hands with his mind. Then his mind quit.

5

Awareness returned as a needle penetrated his arm. Daniel explored the sting with his fingers and discovered that a thin tube had entered his left arm. When he drew his hand back, it snagged in wires that stretched across his chest. He reached to his eyes to clear his vision, and found a mist washing over his face. A mask seemed to be producing the haze, so he pulled it away.

A hand pushed the mask tighter against his face. "This will help you breathe better," a female voice said. "Dr. Jacobsen would you come please"

In a few seconds, a woman's face pressed close to his. "Mr. Nordal, can you hear me?"

I am not deaf. Daniel nodded.

"I am Dr. Jacobsen. You were brought to the Lillesand clinic. We have arranged to send you to the hospital in Arendal, but first we want to make you a little more comfortable. Okay?"

No, it is not okay. He tried to sit.

Dr. Jacobsen gently pressed his shoulders back. "It is best that you rest for now."

"No hospital," Daniel said, and tried to sit again.

"Karin, I need your help here. Now!"

Hands grasped both of his arms. Something cold and wet wiped his arm. He saw a third person holding a syringe. By twisting abruptly, Daniel managed to free his arms.

"Let him be," Dr. Jacobsen said. "Mr. Nordal, we are not going to make you do anything, but you must understand that you are very sick." The doctor shook her head. "If you do not cooperate, it will be difficult for us to help you."

"I am not . . . going to Arendal."

"No one will force you to go, but you should be watched for a few days. In Arendal you could see a specialist." She leaned forward and looked into Daniel's eyes. "You cannot afford to have another episode like this."

"No, I just . . . forgot my . . . inhaler . . . I will be . . . fine."

Dr. Jacobsen argued at length, and in vain. When she learned that Daniel lived alone on an island, she insisted that he stay with someone in town.

Someone turned off the overhead lights, and Daniel was left alone to inhale the mist. He felt his chest lighten in inverse proportion to the pain in his head. After a few minutes, Ingrid came into the room.

"How . . . did . . . you . . . know?"

"Oh my God, do not try to talk." She repeated Dr. Jacobsen's plea to go to Arendal, but Daniel just shook his head. In the end, she said that Daniel should stay at her apartment for a few days.

Four hours later, the clinic staff helped him into Ingrid's Volvo. As soon as the car was underway he asked, "Would you . . . stop at . . . the Hotel Norge?" Her head whipped around and gave him a look that silenced him for the rest of the trip.

Daniel coughed and napped, and coughed and napped into the following morning. Twenty-four hours after he left the clinic, Ingrid told him about the rescue. "You have Eric Haugen to thank. He stopped a passing car and they rushed you to the clinic. Dr. Jacobsen believes that Eric saved your life."

"I must find him as soon as possible, and thank him." He set down a mug of chicken broth. "I wonder why he would work for Birk?"

"Oh, stop it! Maybe he just needs to make a little money. Drink the broth."

"Do you know what happened to my boat?"

"You can thank Eric for that too. It was being carried out on the tide, but he brought it ashore before it could sink."

"Sink?"

"The transom Daniel. It held together just long enough." She poured more broth. "Eric called the marina, and that is how I knew you were in trouble. About the marina—I have work to do this afternoon. Are you well enough to be left alone?"

Daniel nodded, and then he buried his face in his hands. "I have to have a boat." He raised his head suddenly. "Oh my God, I have to talk with Laura Olsen."

She shook a finger at him. "Dr. Jacobsen told you to rest; we can talk about these things tomorrow."

As soon as Ingrid left, Daniel called for a taxi and went directly to the Hotel Norge. It was a gamble, he knew. He might not be able to talk alone with Laura; maybe she left the country, and if he asked the clerk to call their room, he risked being sent away. There was no choice; he must go directly to their room. Daniel saw an elderly couple registering at the front desk, so he slipped passed them and walked directly to the stairs. It was room 203, he remembered. The stairs proved more difficult than he expected, so by the time he reached the second floor he was exhausted and wheezing. By leaning against the wall, he was able to regain control of his breathing, so he inched to Birk's door and knocked.

Laura opened the door with Robert at her side. "Mr. Nordal, what a surprise." She smiled briefly, and then her mouth fell open. Robert dashed behind his mother.

"Who's that?" Birk asked.

Daniel realized at once that he had failed. He slumped against the door frame, and felt a weariness he had never known sweep over him. There was no point in talking now; he was too tired. So very tired.

"It's Mr. Nordal," Laura said in a loud voice. "Are you all right?" She stepped aside as Birk came to the door.

"God, the man is drunk," Birk said. "Look here, you have no business—"

"No!" Daniel took a deep breath. "I came to warn you."

"You warn me? Get out of here."

Daniel turned to Laura. "A child died at the island because the current is strong."

Birk took a step closer. "I said get out of here."

"You're scaring Robert," Laura said. "Maybe we should listen."

"I know a drunk when I see one." Birk pressed the door against Daniel, and pushed him into the hallway. "If you come back I'll call the police."

Daniel sat on the stairs and used his inhaler. He could hear Birk and Laura's raised voices seeping into the hallway. Linda's scream at the cove entered his consciousness, and he tried to block it by pressing his hands against his ears, and by forcing his mind back to the present. He would need a boat as soon as possible. After five minutes, he felt that he could walk. The bank was close by, and by walking slow he knew he would manage.

The regular deposits set up by Anna Olsen had been stopped. He withdrew eight thousand crowns, the balance of the account. With the money shoved in his pocket, he walked away coughing. He would have to wait until Ingrid returned from the marina to ask about repairing his boat. In the meantime, the harbour was close and he wanted to thank Eric. So he set out along the waterfront, but unable to find the old seaman, Daniel settled onto a bench and let the sound of lapping water calm him. Soon, his head nodded and he yielded to sleep.

"Mr. Nordal," he heard, or perhaps his mind was playing tricks.

"Mr. Nordal," but this time with a touch on his arm. It sounded like Laura. A memory from the hotel room? A gentle shake. Daniel straightened his aching neck and looked about. There she was, sitting on the bench beside him.

"I'm sorry to bother you, but just after you left and Birk took Robert to find ice cream, your friend Ingrid called. She told me how sick you were and you were missing, and she knew you wanted to talk with me. Of course I told her you had been to the hotel." She turned to look out over the water. "Well, I thought I would come to the waterfront and look. She's worried; I think you should call her."

Daniel wiped at his eyes with his sleeve. "I am doing very well, and you are very kind to look for me. There are only a few places in Lillesand I could be. Ingrid will be here soon."

"You must think my husband is unkind, but you don't know him as I do. He deals with people that . . . well . . . he has to put on a tough face to survive in his business. This property here is so important to him. It's because of his father you know. You knew his father?"

"Oh yes, I knew him well. We were neighbours on Long Island, but Birk must have been away at that time."

Laura shook her head. "Away is one way to put it. Ole was ashamed of him. He acted like he didn't have a son."

"That does not sound like the man I knew."

"Never tell Birk I told you this, but it may help you to understand him. Birk got into some trouble as a teenager, and he ended up in a juvenile home. When Birk came home, relations with his father were poor. But then, when Ole divorced his mother and married Anna it was all over for them."

"I am a little confused . . ."

"I'm sorry. About this property. Well, Birk saw himself in competition with his father. You know, to be the more successful businessman. Even after Ole died! Now, he sees a chance to develop his father's own property. Right here in his father's homeland. It sounds silly when I say it, but to Birk this is a terribly important matter."

Daniel sat with his elbows resting on his knees. How sad this is, he thought, Birk is competing with a dead man. What about the danger? What about Anna's wishes to leave the land as it was? And what about Linda and Emma's resting place?

Laura looked at Daniel. "Are you all right? Here I am going on and on about Birk, and you had such a loss on the island. It must be very hard for you to think of leaving." She sighed.

"Birk and I talked about the current at the cove. He says it is a simple matter of building a breakwater, and the beach will be as safe as any. I wish he had told you."

Daniel sat up and shrugged. "Has your husband ever developed a beach or built a breakwater? Has he talked with the county officials?" A Volvo stopped close by. "There is Ingrid now."

The following morning, Ingrid agreed to take Daniel to the marina to check on his boat. She introduced him to Karl, the man who had evaluated the damage to his skiff. The boat was on blocks, and the motor was lying beside it on the ground.

Karl pointed to the transom. "Rotten wood here." He shook his head. "The only thing holding it together was the motor clamp."

"What would it cost to replace the transom, and how soon can it be done?"

Karl tipped the boat and pointed to the keel near the stern. "It is more than the transom. Here, can you see the separation? Rebuilding this skiff would be more difficult than building a new one and it would cost more."

After a long discussion with Karl, he concluded that the only short-term solution would be to rent a boat. He could provide the motor, and that would trim the cost. All the rental boats were made of fibreglass, but Ingrid convinced him that it would be easier to handle. Karl mounted his motor on a rented boat, but Daniel insisted on transferring his own oars. "They fit my hands." He slid into the stern seat and started the motor.

"And what are you doing?" Ingrid asked. "You are not well enough to go out on the water."

"I am certainly well enough to go back to the cabin. Even to row the whole way if I choose."

Ingrid stood on the edge of the seawall with arms folded. "If you leave now, do not ever look to me for help again. Ever!"

Daniel sighed. "Very well, for your sake."

"What is the matter with you? For my sake? You almost died. That island will stay where it is for another day. You know Daniel; I am tired of hearing about the damn island."

"Why not for your sake? You have been a good friend."

"Maybe the only friend you have." She pulled her braid over her shoulder and yanked it. "You cannot bring anyone back by staying on that island."

"You cannot expect me to turn my back . . ."

"Things change with time. Can you see that?" She started to unravel her braid.

"I just want to see how the boat handles," he said in a low voice.

"Oh, do whatever the hell you want. Go swim to the island." She flung her braid to her back, turned and walked away.

Daniel was a few minutes from the marina when the motor sputtered and stopped. The fuel tank was full so he attempted to restart the engine. After several attempts, he considered that the cylinder head might be flooded with fuel, so he waited while the boat twisted and bobbed on the chop. After several minutes he tried but failed to get even a cough from the motor. If he was going to row back to the marina, he realized he would have to do it at once before he drifted further from land. So he used the inhaler, set the oars, and started to pull.

The whine of a motor caught his attention. He turned and saw a launch approach, with Karl at the wheel. It turned sharply in front of him and cut power. "Having trouble with the motor? Come on back with me and I will take a look." Karl threw a line that Daniel secured to the bow cleat.

As soon as he could, Daniel climbed from the boat, and without a word, walked away. Karl was talking with Ingrid; they both turned to look at him. He walked along the harbour toward the village centre. Though he was sure he heard his name, he did not want to talk. He wanted to walk. Past the Lillesand church, he turned east. The exertion caused him to cough, but he adjusted his pace to ease the symptoms. As he walked, the murk in his mind started to clear.

Why did I walk away? Ingrid was only trying to help. Could Ingrid be right? Maybe there was nothing more to do. Then he thought of his wife and child swept away to their death, and to give up would be disloyal. No, he could not give up. He plodded on until he left the city and passed a campground and a farmhouse. The questions he asked himself continued to haunt him even as he tried to suppress them.

Just past a campground, he became overwhelmed with fatigue. As he turned to go back, he saw Ingrid's Volvo creep along the shoulder of the road. She pulled onto the road, drove past him and turned. Ingrid pushed open the passenger door from the inside, and he entered. Neither of them talked about what happened at the marina. It was as if Daniel routinely walked out of town, and arranged for Ingrid to pick him up. She told him that his motor required repairs, and it would take a couple of days to get parts. "If you want to go to the island, I will take you if that is your wish, but you are welcome to stay with me until the motor is fixed. You could use a little more time to heal."

"If it is not too much trouble. One more day." Daniel sighed. "A part of me wants to fight what Birk wants to do, but a part of me is unsure."

"It must be difficult for you."

"I wonder if Solveig—"

"Oh yes, Solveig. She called me today, and invited us to come to Lyngør this Saturday. Maybe if you are feeling better? Solveig is very anxious to show us the property she bought."

And maybe she will have found something out about Birk, Daniel thought.

6

Daniel went to the island as soon as Karl repaired his motor. He inspected the cabin and cove; there was no sign of recent activity. Before he could travel with Ingrid to Lyngør, he needed to be convinced that Birk was not an immediate threat. The promise of information from Solveig outweighed his fear of leaving, so he decided to go.

Early Saturday morning, they rode in Ingrid's Volvo to the marina at Gjeving, and took the first ferry of the day. It was at Holmen—one of the four islands of Lyngør—that they went ashore to Solveig's threatening hug. In Solveig's shadow, shivering and stamping her feet, was a slender girl who appeared to Daniel to be ten years old. After many sighs, and a resounding "yes," Solveig introduced the dark-haired girl as "Sarah, the young lady I told you about." Daniel searched his memory without success, but took his cue from Ingrid who seemed to know about her.

Solveig led them along a paved path that climbed a hill,

meandered past a schoolhouse, and took them to a footbridge to the island Odden. She talked steadily about the tourist traffic in the summer. "People love to turn back the clock you know. This village has remained unchanged since the days of sailing ships, and the absence of cars is a novelty of course." Ingrid stayed close to Solveig and nodded at regular intervals. Daniel trailed several paces behind the women, and Sarah shuffled along in the rear.

Solveig's cottage was along the seawall that faced the Lyngør Sound. It was white with a red tile roof, as were most of the village buildings. A previous owner had created two apartments. Solveig explained that she would convert the sitting room of the downstairs apartment into a speciality shop where she would sell sweaters, silver jewellery, and souvenirs. The upstairs apartment would serve as her living space during the tourist season.

Sarah stood frowning, with her arms folded, while the two women chatted by the cottage entrance. Daniel felt an urgent need to cheer Sarah, so he approached her. "How do you like Lyngør?" was all he could think of to say. She gave him a sideways glance, but said nothing.

"Oh Daniel," Solveig said. "Sarah does not understand Norwegian."

"Then it is no wonder she frowns. We all need to speak English when she is around."

Solveig's mouth fell open, and Ingrid cocked her head to

one side and gave a weak smile. Daniel repeated his question in English.

"Bor-ing," Sarah said.

"I wonder if they sell ice cream at the restaurant by the ferry dock," Daniel said.

"Yes," Solveig said. "The Blue Lantern has ice cream."

Daniel turned to Sarah. "Are you interested?" Sarah gave a barely perceptible nod, and Solveig shrugged when Daniel turned his head to her.

As Daniel walked away with Sarah, he heard Solveig talk to Ingrid in Norwegian. "I am not very good with children. But Daniel? I am surprised. Oh, but I forget—Emma was Sarah's age when she . . ." She sighed. "I hope he will be all right."

"Maybe this is good for him," he heard Ingrid reply, and then he could hear no more.

What were they talking about? Sarah is in a strange place with strange people. It should be obvious that she would need extra attention.

"I think you would like it here in the summer," Daniel said.

Sarah twisted her face into a lopsided frown. "There's nothing to do."

"In the summer there will be many people here, and some will be your age."

"Yeah."

He remembered that he would have been overjoyed to explore the island alone when he was a boy. "Are you through with school for the year?"

"No."

When they came to the footbridge that led to Holmen, Daniel stopped and they looked down at the boats in the waterway. "In Norway, someone your age would be learning to handle a boat. Does that interest you?"

"Girls?"

"Of course. Ingrid has a fine sailboat. She has been sailing since she was your age."

Sarah lifted her head, and her frown faded away. "Really?"

At last, Daniel thought. "She not only sails, but she builds boats too." They continued over the bridge. "When we get back to the cottage, I think Ingrid would love to tell you all about it."

The Blue Lantern was wedged between a cliff, which formed part of its back wall, and the sea. Sarah and Daniel made a selection from the freezer and ate on the deck that extended over the Sound.

"How did you come to be here with Solveig?" Daniel asked.

"My dad has business in Oslo. He wanted me to come and meet Solveig." Sarah's mouth puckered as if she tasted something sour. "He wanted me to spend time with her. Without him."

"Did you like Oslo?"

"No."

He pitched his ice cream in a waste container when Sarah turned to look at a swan. "Is there anything in Norway that you like?"

"I hate it here. I wish I was home."

"When my family moved to America, I hated everything too. Maybe because everything was new and strange, but maybe because it was not my choice to move. But time changed that."

"You came back here, didn't you?"

"Maybe we should get back to Ingrid and Solveig." Sarah finished her ice cream as they slowly walked back to the cottage. They talked about pets they have had, books they had read, and places they had seen. When they walked into the cottage, they were still chatting.

"Well would you look at that. Sarah is not frowning," Solveig said in Norwegian. "Sarah seems to have found a friend."

"Please remember to speak English," Daniel said. He turned to Ingrid. "Sarah would love to talk with you about boating. While you two are talking, perhaps Solveig would like to tell me about her plans for the shop." Ingrid took Sarah to the seawall, while Solveig opened the drapes to let light fill the empty sitting room.

"Can you see the potential?" Solveig waved her arm about.

"There will be display cases for jewellery along this wall, and shelves for sweaters over here."

"I guess you have considered the short selling season." Daniel cleared his throat. "Have you asked your contacts about Birk Olsen?"

"Short profitable seasons can work well. Consider Geiranger. A summer gold mine."

"Is it not true that Geiranger has tour groups, hotels, and cruise ships?" Daniel shrugged. "But I know nothing about business."

"Yes, there is less traffic here." Solveig smiled and waved her hand. "But there is no competition."

"Why do you suppose there is no competition? Have you any word about Birk?"

"There is so much work here for a good carpenter. Would you give this some more thought?'

"Yes, but I have obligations."

"There is plenty of time to decide. I do not expect to open the shop until next year." Solveig walked around the room and looked at imaginary fixtures from different angles. "Natural pine with a high gloss would look best."

Why should Solveig get involved with my problem? She has not contacted anyone, he decided. Naturally, her mind is full of details about her shop. Of course, she would not remember. He should have stayed on the island. There is no telling what Birk was up to.

"You do not seem well," Solveig said. "Are you all right?"

"No I do not feel so good. Maybe a walk will help."

Solveig followed him outside. "Oh, about Birk Olsen, the man you were concerned about. He has a shady reputation. A minor contractor known for shoddy work and big profits. He gets away with certain shortcuts, probably by bribing building inspectors. Once in a while he pays a fine, but in the end it seems that he does what he wants."

Daniel stopped walking, and turned to face her. "How do you know this?"

"Remember, I have a friend in New York. There was an article about corruption in the building industry in Newsday. He said it was easy to find by searching for Birk's name in the paper's archives." Solveig shrugged. "Friends come in handy Daniel."

Daniel thanked her, but decided the information was not useful. It only confirmed his suspicions. He felt the need to get away by himself, and he had to walk. Daniel paced along the seawall, but that did not give him enough room, so he turned onto an unpaved trail that turned inland. When the trail ended in an uninhabited area of Odden, he sat on a boulder and stared at the sea. In a few minutes he felt calm, and thought that this would be a suitable place to live.

When he returned to the seawall, he saw Ingrid, Solveig, and Sarah talking and laughing. As he approached, Ingrid left the group and came to him. "We have a change in plans," she said. We are all going to Lillesand. Solveig and Sarah will stay for the weekend." Ingrid laughed. "Do not look so worried, they will not be staying at your cabin."

Daniel nodded. "Going back is a good decision. I need to keep an eye on things."

Ingrid rolled her eyes. "This is for Sarah, not for you."

Solveig and Sarah came to where they were talking. "Isn't it fantastic?" Sarah asked. "We're going sailing in Ingrid's boat."

"How very generous of Ingrid," Daniel said.

"How very generous of both of us," Ingrid said in Norwegian. "You are coming too." She winked. "Sarah thinks you are cool."

Solveig rubbed her hands together. "Thank you—both of you. It is so important to me that Sarah has a good time."

"Remember to speak English," Daniel said firmly. He turned to Sarah. "Ingrid was saying that she will bring lots of good things to eat. She wants to have a sailing party." He noticed that Ingrid's smile became a little less natural.

They all had dinner at The Kettle in Lillesand, where Solveig and Sarah shared a room. Daniel spent a restless night on the sofa in Ingrid's apartment, and when the sun rose, he decided he would walk along the harbour until the bakery opened.

Daniel stopped at the beach where Eric had come to his aid,

and eased himself onto a bench. Was this an odd- or even-numbered day, he wondered. What would he be doing this morning, if Birk had not come into his life? Everything seemed wrong. Why did he go along with the plans to go sailing today? He tried to lose himself in the play of morning light on the ever-moving water.

A hand touched his shoulder, and it was as if he had dreamed it. At first, he was unsure what was happening, but then he twisted his head around and saw Eric standing behind him. Daniel started to rise, but Eric pressed on his shoulder. "No, just sit and I will join you."

"There is so much to say—" Daniel started.

"There is no need to say anything captain. We do what we can, and it is good to see you looking well." Eric came around the bench and sat next to Daniel. "There is little for me to do these days but sit and think and I have been worrying about you."

"That is very kind, but why do you worry? You hardly know me. Anyway, as you can see, I am breathing just fine . . . thanks to you."

Eric pulled his pipe from his pocket and examined the bowl. "Have you quit the island?"

Daniel twisted his head to look directly at Eric. "Why do you ask?"

"I have worked for many people in my life. Some were ruthless, and one ship's captain—he was mad. But, Birk Olsen is not so bad. Yes, he is a little strange, but not like some I have known. He pays me, and I take him where he wants to go, but I do not report to him what we talk about."

Daniel sighed. "I should be on the island now."

"I wonder Daniel—if Birk went away, would you live on that island forever?"

Daniel looked out to sea. "It looks like good sailing weather. That will please Ingrid."

"Are you going with her? A trip?"

"Just doing her a favour."

Eric raised an eyebrow. "I hope you do not mind some reflections of an old man. Birk will not change the skerries. The wind and sea will erase his mark in time. But Daniel, you already know how fragile people are."

He cannot possibly understand, Daniel thought. He was not there.

At ten in the morning, under a cloudless sky, Daniel met Ingrid, Solveig and Sarah at the marina. "The boat will probably make me sick," Solveig whispered to Daniel. "I am responsible for Sarah, so naturally I must go." Sarah squealed when she saw Ingrid's sloop, and climbed on board without hesitation.

Ingrid assigned everyone a job. Sarah would steer, with Daniel as her coach. Ingrid would tend the sails, and Solveig was to watch the horizon and breathe deeply.

Daniel took the wheel until they were well away from the marina, then he turned it over to Sarah. He explained that she needed to give certain commands before she could change course. Almost as soon as he finished explaining, Sarah spun the wheel without warning; the boat heeled to where the jib touched the sea. Then she released the wheel in fright so that the boat turned into the wind and lost way. Sarah threw herself on the stern bench and sobbed, while Solveig's head disappeared over the gunwale.

Ingrid set loose the jib sheets and started to make her way to the stern, but Daniel held up his hand. "Give us a few minutes." He spoke softly. "There is no harm done Sarah. Everyone who has ever sailed did what you did. But you are lucky to learn this lesson on your first trip. In fact, I was hoping you would do it, so we could see if Ingrid was awake."

"I don't want to sail anymore," Sarah said.

"Give it a little more time. Rest a little, and when you feel ready you can help me with the wheel."

"We better catch some wind," Ingrid said, pointing to Solveig. "Rolling in place is not so good." She backed the jib, and Daniel took the wheel. He coaxed Sarah into taking the wheel again, and he gently overrode some of her decisions that were not compatible with the wind direction. As they sailed, Daniel explained how to determine which way the wind was blowing, and how to use it to her advantage. For the next half hour, Sarah spoke little and worked with her teeth clenched. Then she began to smile, and declined all offers for relief at the wheel.

Solveig, looking pale, declared it was time to go ashore for a picnic. "Let us show Sarah the island where Daniel lives. She would love his little cabin." Daniel tried to think of an alternative, but Sarah's enthusiasm caused him to agree.

When they approached the cabin, Daniel saw that the cabin door was ajar. He lengthened his stride in order to get to the cabin first, but he found no one inside.

"This is cool," Sarah said as she looked around.

"I will make some coffee," Daniel said, and began to count coffee beans until he saw cigarette butts in the sink. Aware of Sarah's presence, he refrained from commenting. "I am going to the cove," Daniel said.

"What is wrong with you?" Ingrid asked in a whisper, and Daniel pointed to the sink.

"Please do not spoil the day for Sarah."

"I will take a little walk before lunch," Daniel said loudly.

"Can we explore?" Sarah asked.

"I will set out the food, while you three look around," Solveig said.

"I am going alone," Daniel hissed in Ingrid's ear.

"I am coming too," Ingrid said flatly. "Come Sarah, let us explore."

On a rise above the cove, Daniel found stakes in the ground with orange ribbons tied to them. There were also ribbons tied to some of the birch trees. He rushed from ribbon to ribbon, yanking stakes from the ground, and pulling ribbons from the trees.

"What's that for?" Sarah asked.

"A visitor was playing games here, and he forgot to clean up," Daniel said.

Ingrid put her hand on Sarah's shoulder. "Look how pretty it is down by the shore."

Ingrid and Sarah scampered down to the water's edge. "It's perfect," Sarah said with her hands to her face. "If this was my island, I would live right here." She looked at the bench and the inscription. "Who are Linda and Emma?"

Ingrid hesitated, but Daniel overheard and came closer carrying a bundle of stakes and a wad of ribbon. "They were people who loved this place, and never wanted to leave." He swallowed hard. "But, they had to go away, so I put their names here." Daniel smiled at Sarah. "Solveig is probably waiting for us. Let us have some lunch." Sarah ran ahead on the trail to the cabin.

Ingrid took Daniel's arm. "Thank you," she said.

Daniel declared that he had no appetite, and he went to the dock to think about what he saw at the cove. He decided that he would check with the county office the next morning to see if the property had changed hands. What if it had? What could he do about it? He stared out over the water feeling lost, until he heard footfalls. Solveig approached carrying a sandwich in a napkin. She sat beside him, and without a word, handed the sandwich to him.

"I am glad you joined me." Daniel accepted the food. "I need some advice." He told her what had happened when he tried to talk with Laura.

"Leave it all behind." Solveig sighed. "That is not the advice you were hoping for, but I want to be honest with you. Eat something Daniel." She waited until he took a bite of food. "Birk Olsen is probably as stubborn as you are."

"Can I do anything about him?"

Solveig laughed. "You just proved my point. If you must continue with this business, you need more information. You should try to contact Anna Olsen. If she says she turned over the island to her stepson, then at least you will know for sure."

"But where can I find her? Birk claims she is in a nursing home, and he is not about to tell me which one. How many nursing homes are there?"

"Start with her last address, and maybe the mail will be sent to her." Solveig shrugged. "You could hire a lawyer to find her if that does not work." A smile crept over her face. "If he is lying to you, all you need to do is call his bluff."

"Call his bluff? Please explain."

7

The sailing party returned to the Lillesand marina when the
sun slid low in the western sky. Because of the late hour, Daniel
spent another night on Ingrid's sofa. In the early morning, he
wrote and rewrote a letter to Anna Olsen, and he was at the
post office as soon as it opened. Then he went to the county
offices, where he confirmed that there was no change in the
property record for the island. He obtained a photocopy of
the record and walked briskly to the nearest public phone.
Daniel called the Hotel Norge, and said he needed to speak
with Mr. Birk Olsen at once. In a few seconds, a sleepy sound-
ing Birk answered the phone.

"Mr. Olsen, this is Daniel Nordal." Birk tried to speak,
but Daniel raised his voice and continued. "I thought it was
fair that I give you warning. Just now I came from the county
administration and it is clear that the registered owner of
the island is Anna Olsen." The phone seemed hot against
his ear. "I have been designated the lawful custodian of the
property." He cleared his throat. "Also, I need to remind you
that disturbing that land is a violation of Norwegian law. If

necessary, I will do everything in my power to stop you." He took a deep breath and cut off Birk's protest. "I have removed the stakes and ribbons that you placed near the cove." Daniel removed the handset from his ear, but he could hear Birk shouting. Then he placed the handset in its cradle and saw his wet handprint. "There, it is done."

It would be at least two hours before Birk came to the island, Daniel estimated. First Birk would have to find Eric, and have the launch brought around to the dock near the hotel. He tried to imagine Birk in a rage, and on the way to the marina, he tried unsuccessfully to feel pleased.

Ingrid was adjusting the stays of a schooner when Daniel arrived. When she saw him, she climbed down from the deck and ran to him. "I have a surprise for you. Come!" She led him behind one of the buildings where several boats were in various stages of repair. Ingrid yanked a tarpaulin from one of the boats. "No fiberglass here. Do you like it?"

Daniel saw a compact sloop with varnished planking and brass fittings. He ran his hand over the hull. "What a beautiful piece of work." He turned to Ingrid. "Did you do this?"

She shook her head. "It would be a fine boat except . . ." She played with her braid. "Well, the mast was not stepped properly. It is too far forward for the design of the hull."

"I do not understand."

"When you take your hand from the tiller of a sailboat,

it should turn into the wind. That would slow or stop the boat."

"Very useful if you fall overboard."

"Exactly. This boat will run before the wind if you release the tiller—it has a lee helm."

"What boat builder would make that mistake?"

"This was not a professional boat builder, but a craftsman who had built several fine skiffs. But, he did not understand sailboat design. The boat was to be for his grandchildren, but of course, it is unsafe. You can see the way the mast is stepped; it could not be moved without rebuilding the keel."

"Are you asking me for advice? If you cannot fix it, I certainly cannot."

"The boat is for sale. Sixteen hundred crowns. Can you believe it? Less than the cost of materials."

Daniel laughed. "Now I see the plot. You want me to have another unsafe boat."

"It would be a perfect motor boat for you. Look, the reinforced transom can take a small outboard, and the daggerboard can be pulled to reduce your draught."

Daniel walked around the boat. "There are oarlocks."

"This boat would be a little too heavy for rowing, especially with your condition. The first thing I would do is cut the mast off. It will reduce the weight, reduce the draught, and give you a lower centre of gravity. And remove the temptation to sail."

He threw his hands up. "An amputation, on such a fine piece of work? It would ruin the lines of the boat. Never! But tell me; is it the new policy of the marina to operate at a loss? I am not asking for a special favour."

Ingrid sighed. "You are impossible. This is not marina business; the builder asked me if I wanted to buy it."

Daniel placed his hands on Ingrid's shoulders. "Thank you for thinking of me. Yes the boat is perfect." Ingrid rose on her toes, and quickly kissed Daniel on the cheek. "I have an appointment to keep. Would it be possible to transfer the motor now?"

Daniel spent an hour motoring in the harbour to check the boat's handling. Under power, it lacked the speed and agility of his skiff, but he liked its solid feel. Pleased with his purchase, Daniel set a course for the island.

A short distance from the mouth of the harbour he spotted Eric's launch approaching off his port bow. So, they have already been to the island, Daniel concluded. Birk must have been in a rage not to find him there. The approaching boat did not slow, nor was there any sign of acknowledgement from the wheelhouse. Of course, they would not recognize his new boat. Daniel altered his course to come closer, and just as the boat passed, Eric turned to look. The launch slowed, and there was a blast from its horn, but Daniel faced straight ahead, maintaining his course and speed. The dub-dub-dub of the launch's engine changed pitch and grew louder. In the edge of his vision he could see that Eric's boat had turned and was about to overtake him.

The bow wave of the launch caused his boat to roll, so he could no longer pretend to be unaware. Birk appeared on the foredeck, frowning and waving. Eric matched the smaller boat's speed and Birk shouted something that Daniel could not hear clearly over the engine noise. Birk shouted to Eric and the engine noise abruptly subsided.

"I want to talk with you," Birk said leaning over the rail.

Daniel understood, but he cupped his hand behind his ear and shook his head.

"Stop!"

Daniel raised one of his hands, palm upward, and he forced a quizzical look on his face.

The launch, with power cut, fell behind, while Birk stood on the foredeck and beat his hands against the rail. At once, the launch accelerated and passed Daniel. Its wake caused the smaller boat to roll almost to the gunwale. Daniel turned the boat to take the waves on his bow. "I will see you shortly Birk," he said to the wind.

Soon after the launch passed from view, the motor sputtered and died. His suspicion was confirmed when he checked the fuel tank. He had spent an hour motoring around the harbour, he remembered. Of course, a heavy boat will burn fuel quickly. But he had thought to load his oars. He set the oars, and used his inhaler in anticipation of heavy exertion. If he paced himself, he reasoned, he would be okay. Birk could wait. It would be a lesson in patience for him. He pulled on the oars, and concluded that he had never tried to row a more difficult boat. Daniel yanked the daggerboard from its well to reduce drag, but he could feel no difference.

In a couple of minutes, he felt the need to use the inhaler again. After rowing for a few more minutes, he had to repeat the process. In spite of the medicine, his chest felt heavy and his hands started to shake. He could drift and catch the attention of the next boat he saw. That would certainly be a topic of conversation around the harbour. Did you hear about the fool who ran out of fuel and was too weak to row a small boat? But the boat has sails. So what if it had a lee helm. He was not going to drop the tiller; he was not a child. Daniel understood boats.

Daniel quickly unpacked and rigged the sails. He inserted the daggerboard, and with one hand gripping the tiller, he pulled in the jib sheets until the wind filled the sail. The boat heeled at once and was underway. Pressure against the tiller was different from what he was accustomed to, but he adjusted quickly. Pleased with how smoothly the boat sailed, Daniel was able to relax. Ingrid overstated the problem, he concluded. He would stay alert, and all would be well.

When the island came in view, he could see Eric's launch and a figure pacing the shoreline. Daniel wanted to come to the dock smartly, to spill the air at just the right moment, but he had never practised the manoeuvre with that boat. Fearing that he might crash into the dock, he tried to think of a different, yet dramatic arrival. There was a sandy spit near the dock. He would direct the boat onto the sand at just the right speed for a smooth grounding. Daniel imagined his arrival—stepping from the boat with dignity and dealing head-on with Birk.

The distance and heading were right. He secured the boom, and set the jib sheets free; the speed dropped just as he expected. It would be perfect. Just as the bow slid onto the spit, he remembered the daggerboard; a second later, he heard the sound of tearing wood, the boat stopped and Daniel fell forward. In less than a second, he felt the impact of the mast against his left shoulder, then more slowly—the pain. The daggerboard had arrested the boat's progress onto the spit, so it began to drift from the shore. At once Eric waded into the water, grabbed hold of the bow, and eased the boat onto the sand.

"Are you okay?" Eric asked.

No, he thought, I am not okay. My confidence and my boat damaged. Daniel pushed back from the mast and explored his shoulder with his hand. "Just a bruise." He rose like a man of advanced age, and stepped gingerly onto the sand. "You come to my rescue again, and again I thank you." He placed his hand on Eric's shoulder. "We should go to the cabin so you can dry off. I will start a fire."

"What's he saying?" Birk shouted.

"You have put Birk in a very ugly mood," Eric said in a low voice.

Daniel insisted on starting a fire in the stove before he would talk with Birk. While Eric attempted to dry himself, Birk paced the floor and muttered to himself.

Daniel fingered a folded piece of paper in his pocket, and wondered if he could really fool Birk. He would have to do more than fool him—he would have to push Birk to where he would reveal his lies. What if Birk had been telling the truth? But no, that was impossible. It was time to do it. He took a deep breath and pulled the paper from his pocket. Daniel unfolded the copy of the property record and cleared his throat.

"I will come to the point," Daniel said firmly. "The document in my hand designates me as the sole legal occupant of this island. That was the arrangement made by Anna Olsen, which she recorded in the county records." He rolled the paper into a tube and waved it at the doorway. "It was also her wish that this land remain in a natural state."

Birk laughed. "What are you talking about? Let me see that." He snapped the paper from Daniel and unrolled it. "It's in Norwegian." He shoved it back. "Read it to me just the way it's written."

Daniel swallowed hard. "It is full of legal terms. I cannot translate word for word."

Birk grabbed the paper again and thrust it at Eric. "What does it say?" Eric's lips moved as he read the paper to himself, while Birk kept a steady gaze on Daniel. Eric glanced at Daniel and shook his head.

"You have nerve; I give you credit," Eric said in Norwegian.

"What?" Birk twisted around to look at Eric.

Eric shrugged. "I am a seaman, not a lawyer." He returned the paper to Daniel.

Daniel wadded the paper in a pocket, and folded his arms. "There it is Mr. Olsen. Now, if you wish to explain your situation here."

"I don't have to explain anything to you. I came all the way out here for this nonsense? You know who the authorities should be interested in?" He shook a finger at Daniel. "You! And about those survey markers that you pulled—you cost me time and money. I intend to be compensated." He turned to Eric. "Let's get the hell out of here." Birk strode from the cabin.

Daniel grabbed Eric's arm. "Now I owe you for many things."

"Do not expect me to do this again."

Birk came back to the doorway. "I said, let's go."

"In the end you are making things more difficult for yourself." Eric said in Norwegian. "I must go."

As soon as he was alone, Daniel pulled the paper from his pocket, crumbled it, and thrust it into the stove. He replayed

Birk's reaction in his mind, and he could find no comfort. Had his bluff really failed, or was Birk more skilled at playing the game? He looked at the photograph of the woman and child through wet eyes. If I have made a fool of myself, he thought, it is of no concern. I must keep trying. His thoughts turned to finding Anna Olsen. Anna grew up in Lillesand; there must be someone who writes to her. The idea gave him hope, so he left the cabin and went directly to his boat.

He gathered up the pieces of daggerboard that had washed ashore, and threw them in the boat. An easy job for Ingrid, he decided.

Without a daggerboard, the boat was difficult to handle. He reefed the sails, and set a course that allowed for leeward drift. At last, the boat wallowed into the harbour and approached the marina. He secured the boat to a cleat on the seawall, and threw the pieces of daggerboard on shore just as Ingrid approached.

"What is the best way to go about finding someone?" Daniel asked. He waited for a response, but Ingrid only glared at him. "Anna must have had friends."

"I should never have told you about that boat."

"What is wrong?" He looked at the pieces of daggerboard. "Oh, of course I will pay for repairs, and if you would rather not—"

"You should never have sailed that boat, but that is my fault. What was I thinking?"

"A small thing Ingrid. What can a daggerboard cost?"

"It is not the cost." She shook her head. "You just do not see it. Do you?"

"What should I see?" Daniel spread his arms. "I ran out of gas and—"

"Yes, because you cannot think about anything except that island."

"It is not so simple." Daniel sighed. "I need your help Ingrid, and not for the daggerboard. Please? There must be someone in Lillesand who writes to Anna Olsen."

Ingrid thrust her head forward. "No, I cannot help you. I cannot deal with you." Tears filled her eyes. She spun around, and walked away with her hands to her face. After a few paces she stopped and stood still. Without turning her head she said in a hoarse voice, "The Olsens were a prominent family, there should be newspaper articles." Then Ingrid walked away, and though Daniel called to her, she did not stop again.

Though his mind was excited at her suggestion, he felt like something just died in his gut. For a moment, he considered going after her, but then he thought it would be best to wait until she had calmed, and he had checked the newspaper archives. He thought he heard a voice say, "You are a fool Daniel," but he shook his head and walked briskly toward Lillesand centre.

He took the next bus to Kristiansand, and arrived at the

newspaper offices just thirty minutes before closing. With assistance from a woman who kept looking at her watch, he managed to find a reference to Anna Olsen.

Anna was one of the celebrants at her mother's fiftieth wedding anniversary; a celebration held ten years ago. Anna had a younger sister, Marta Gabrielsen, described as a life-long resident of Lillesand.

Daniel took the hand of the startled attendant. "There is hope!"

8

The bus from Kristiansand arrived at Lillesand bus station just as the shadows were merging to a homogeneous grey. Daniel decided he would start searching for Anna's sister first thing in the morning. Rather than spend the night at the island he would cover himself with a tarp, and sleep in his boat. He regretted not tying up his boat closer to the town center. From the bus station, he would have to walk around the harbour to the marina. After walking a short distance, he realized it would be a long time before he would be able to sleep. So, he turned toward the shore, intending to sit on a bench and think. There was just enough light to make out the form of a bench along the seawall.

Daniel was just twenty yards from the bench, when he stopped abruptly. Above the backrest was the unmistakable outline of the watch cap and elfin ears of Eric Haugen. Not in a mood to talk with anyone, Daniel attempted to walk away as silently as possible. Without turning his head, Eric called out, "This is a strange time of day to see you by the harbour Daniel Nordal."

"Eric Haugen? Oh, is that you there?"

"Can you see all right? Come and sit with me."

"How could you tell I was behind you?" Daniel asked as he sat next to Eric.

Eric laughed. "Nothing magical. I looked around a few minutes ago and saw you turn from the street where the light is better. Naturally, I thought you saw me, but I have been here for a while so my eyes have adjusted. Maybe you wanted to be alone?"

"Oh no, of course not Eric."

"Do not worry about offending me. Your face has a different message."

Daniel surveyed the lights on the water. "In another month the harbour will be full of boats."

"Surely you have not come to the harbour to do a survey."

Daniel turned to Eric and began to see the details of his face. He expected to see Eric's lips turned up in a smirk or some indication of sarcasm. All he saw was honesty. What is the matter with me, he thought. This man saved my life, but I am suspicious.

"Forgive me," Eric said, "there are times when I want to be alone too." He started to stand.

Daniel pulled on Eric's sleeve and gently guided him down to the bench. "Being alone has become a habit. Your life as a seaman must have been so different; always surrounded by shipmates in close quarters."

"No Daniel, it would be hard to find a more lonely existence. On watch, it is just you and the sea. Most often, your cabin mate is on duty when you are off. And, I think the sea attracts people who say they like living that way, but I am not so sure." Eric removed his cap and ran his hands through his hair. "I am certain; many seamen do not like their life."

"Then why do they go to sea?"

"Hmmm, that is hard to explain. It is safe. Not from physical danger, but maybe from life."

"Life can be hard."

"Of course, of course. You understand this better than most. You have lost so much." Eric pulled his cap over his head. "I have never had anything to lose. I wonder, is that good or bad?" The two men sat in silence for a minute. "I wonder, would you go to sea if you could?"

Daniel sighed, and spoke in a barely audible voice. "I am at sea."

"Are you staying in town tonight? I have an extra cot in my room."

"Yes, but I have made arrangements. Thank you. I must be going now."

"I will see you on your island tomorrow. You will be there? Oh forgive me, I did not tell you. Birk Olsen has hired me to take him there; he wants to leave at noon."

"What? Again? Now what is he up to?"

"He did not tell me why, except that he wants to talk

with you. He seems... upset. But, since you are in town, would you want to meet with him here? Maybe even tonight?"

Daniel stood abruptly. "No, he can come to me."

There seemed to be no position that Daniel could assume that would allow him sleep. The boat bobbed easily on the chop, and Daniel looked along the mast as it traced arcs through the stars, and his mind raced from problem to problem. How could he begin to trace Marta Gabrielsen if he had to run to the island with every one of Birk's whims? What kind of trouble is he bringing now? Maybe Anna's sister would not be any help after all. Daniel was not running from life, like Eric's seamen. Why did Eric bring it up? He means well. Daniel pulled himself up on the stern bench and laid his head on his knees. The same questions and doubts recycled through his mind without resolution. When he could stand no more, Daniel decided to try Ingrid's sloop.

As expected, there was no lock on the cabin door, and he collapsed at once on a cushioned bench along the bulkhead. In a few seconds, Daniel was asleep.

Daniel woke in a panic. The light intensity in the sloop's cabin told him it was long after sunrise. He stumbled onto the after-deck and saw Ingrid standing by his boat holding a wooden panel in her hand. Daniel swung over the gunwale to the seawall and called to her. She did not respond but threw down what she had in her hand. "I did not think you would mind if I slept in your boat. Last night—"

"Here is your daggerboard." She nodded to the panel on the ground. "I used the broken board as a template. See if it fits."

"There is no need. If you made it, it fits. You are angry that I slept on your boat?"

"I am angry at myself. I only made the daggerboard because I know you well enough. You will sail without it, because you are not thinking anymore, and it will be my fault." She picked up the daggerboard and held it out to Daniel. "See if it fits."

He took the board, leaned over his boat, and slid the board into its well. "Of course, a perfect fit. How much do I owe you for this?"

Ingrid shook her head. "Come, there is coffee in the office, and you can tell me why you had to sleep in my boat."

They sat at a small table and drank coffee while Daniel spoke of his trip to Kristiansand. He told her that Birk wanted to meet him at midday, but did not mention his meeting with Eric. "So, my search for Anna's sister cannot start yet. And I need a plan—how to find her."

Ingrid stood and took the telephone directory from the top of a filing cabinet. "Here is your plan. There; Gabrielsen, Marta." She placed the directory in front of Daniel and stepped out of the office.

Marta's address was in a residential neighbourhood

across the harbour from the marina. Daniel called the number, and to his surprise, was talking with her after just one ring. He claimed to be an old friend of Anna, and asked if he could visit. Marta said she lived alone, and was reluctant to have a stranger come to her house. She was polite, but cut the conversation short.

Daniel went outside and told Ingrid what happened. "Wait here," Ingrid said, and went back to the office. In five minutes, she emerged with a grin on her face. "Marta Gabrielsen will have us over for coffee tomorrow afternoon."

"How did you do that?"

"Do you have time before you go to meet Birk?"

"Yes, a little. But, how did you do that?"

"Good! I have done a favour for you, now I would like one in return."

"Of course Ingrid."

She took hold of his elbow and guided him toward the seawall. "I have a question. I want you to really listen, and to answer honestly. Okay?"

Daniel nodded, and they sat together on the grass by the harbour's edge.

Ingrid sighed. "It is hard to see you struggle like this." She put a hand on his shoulder. "Tell me, what will you do if you learn that Birk has a right to the island?"

Daniel shifted his position and stared out over the water. "He cannot be allowed to develop the island."

A furrow appeared in Ingrid's brow. "You did not answer me."

"I cannot be sure. I will take each day as it comes."

"Owning the island does not give him the right to develop it."

Daniel pulled a clump of grass loose, and threw it in the water. "He will act first, and his lawyers will take care of the rest."

Ingrid let go of his shoulder. "How do you know this? Anyway, if he acts as you say, there are many people in this community that would protest. You can be sure of it."

Daniel snapped his head around to look at her. "He has a small child. There are dangerous currents there. You know what happened."

"Listen to me." She lowered her voice to almost a whisper. "There are hundreds, maybe thousands of places along the coast and in the skerries where families vacation and swim. You grew up here; you know that many places are dangerous. There are always warnings about swimming where there are no beaches or supervision. But, even in supervised swimming pools we hear about tragedy" She touched his hand. "I am sorry Daniel, but you have warned Birk. You have done your duty. You cannot expect everyone to listen to you"

Daniel pulled his hand away from hers, and brought both hands to cover his face. "What you say makes sense in my head, but not in my heart. I know you mean to help—you have been a good friend."

She leaned forward to rest her arms against her knees. "Before you knew Birk existed, did you have a plan to leave the island some day?" Ingrid turned her head to look at him.

Daniel took his hands from his face, and looked at his watch. "I had better leave now, if I am to get to the island before Birk."

When Daniel arrived at the island, he saw that Eric's launch was just a minute behind him. If there was to be a confrontation with Birk, he did not want it to be at the dock. The cabin would be the place where Daniel was most comfortable. He raced to the top of the bluff, and darted into the cabin; as he did so, he felt a familiar heaviness in his chest. He fumbled in his pockets for his inhaler, took two inhalations, sat on the sofa, and picked up an old newspaper.

Birk did not knock. He pushed open the door so that it slammed against the stop. With a scowl on his face, he walked to where Daniel sat, and stood in front of him with folded arms. Eric brushed past Birk, and said in Norwegian, "Are you not feeling well?"

"What're you saying?" Birk asked.

"I just need a minute or two." If I can stay calm, Daniel thought. "Maybe I will make coffee."

"What's he saying?"

Eric did not answer, but went to put a pot of water on the alcohol burner.

"Thank you Eric, I will do the rest."

Birk slammed his fist down on the table. "Speak English!"

Daniel walked slowly to the pantry and took down his crock of coffee beans. "Birk seems overly excited today, but as you can see I must stay relaxed."

"Be careful," Eric said. "Birk is spending a great deal of time and energy. He must be very sure of himself."

"A fool would waste time and energy." He counted the coffee beans into the hopper. Daniel turned his head to look at Birk and spoke English. "When two men talk, they may use the language that suits them. What we said is our business. I said what I had to say to you the last time you were here."

A high-pitched laugh came from Birk's throat that blended eerily with the crunching of the coffee mill. Birk reached into his pocket and produced a wad of paper that he threw on the table. "This is why I'm here."

Daniel added the ground coffee to the water that was starting to simmer. Then he looked at the paper, turned his eyes to Birk, and looked back to the paper again. "Would you like some coffee Eric? Mr. Olsen?"

After a minute of silence, Birk grabbed at the paper, and smoothed it out with his hand. "Look at it!"

Daniel adjusted the flame on the burner. "We do not want this to boil over." He walked to the table and looked down on the paper. He recognized a copy of the ownership record for the island. Each line had been translated into handwritten English. As Daniel looked, he felt his gut turn to stone. He looked up at Birk and shrugged, and then he went to the stove and poured some coffee into a mug. "I cannot wait, the rest can boil longer." He took the mug, sat at the table, and sipped the steaming coffee.

"Who'd have thought you'd try to pull something like this." Birk shook his head and forced a laugh. "For just a little bit, I had my doubts. Daniel, the faithful one—loyal to old Anna. Yes, and protector of the environment. And, you tried to manipulate my wife—using my son's safety as a pretext." He picked up the paper, shook it in Daniel's face and threw it down again. "You're a liar, and a fake. You just want to stay here in your own little world. Isn't that right? Whatever your problem is, you can be damn sure it's not going to be mine."

Daniel felt pain in his left hand from spilled coffee, but he would not move or speak. In his mind, he jumped to his feet and threw Birk from the cabin. In his mind, he screamed and raged at the world. He heard Eric suggest to Birk that maybe it was best to leave him alone.

"So what am I going to do with you?" Birk asked. "We keep butting heads over this island. What is it you want from me?"

Daniel wanted Birk to go away, but he knew there was nothing gained by telling him. He smelled burning coffee, and watched Eric turn off the burner. What had Ingrid advised? To be civil and work something out with Birk? No, it is too late for that. It is too late for anything.

"Mr. Olsen, I have tried to take good care of this property for your family."

"I consider this property in jeopardy as long as you are here."

Daniel slammed the mug on the table and stood suddenly. *No more.* "If I wanted to harm this property you would be standing in ashes." He took a deep breath. *I tried.* "My transgression does not excuse *you.* There is nothing more to discuss with you unless you want to show me proof of ownership."

"You're some character all right. Who are you to ask for proof? This island is the business of the Olsen family, not yours." Birk shook a finger at Daniel. "You told me about Norwegian law? I know all about it. Yes, you can walk on this island, but you cannot live in this building. My lawyers are taking care of what proof I need for the county, but I do not need to give proof to you."

Daniel leaned forward until his face was a few inches from Birk. "I have permission to be here from the owner listed on that paper."

"Where does it say that? Do you have proof?" Birk backed away.

"I . . . have . . . her . . . word." Daniel pushed closer.

Birk backed toward the door. "Are you hard of hearing? I represent the family now. My stepmother is no longer involved.

I've been far too generous with you." He motioned for Eric to join him. "I want you out of here today." Birk spun around and left the cabin with Eric.

9

Daniel met Ingrid at the marina at two in the afternoon, and they rode together in her car to a little red cottage that overlooked Lillesand harbour. Marta Gabrielsen, a slender woman with grey hair fixed in a bun, gave them a warm welcome. Ingrid and Daniel were ushered into a room filled with thickly upholstered furniture. Heavy curtains covered all of the windows, so that Daniel felt he was in a plush cave. Every horizontal surface contained porcelain figures of children, animals, and birds. Marta welcomed them, and served Ingrid and Daniel each a heart shaped waffle served on china.

At first, they talked about how much Lillesand had changed, and then Daniel turned the conversation to his relationship with the Olsen family. He explained that he was living on their island property, but he deduced from Marta's lack of reaction that she already knew. After taking a deep breath, he inquired about Anna.

"Anna, like all of us, is growing old and she cannot do what she would like," Marta said. She passed a tray of waffles, though neither Ingrid nor Daniel had taken a bite of what they had.

"Does she write to you?" Daniel asked.

"Yes. Well, she tries. From the looks of her writing, she can hardly hold a pen."

"Does she write about her stepson?"

Daniel felt a pinch on his thigh. "Slow down," Ingrid whispered from behind a cup at her lips.

"You know, I never met Birk," Marta said. "It would be nice to meet him, but I suppose he is busy. Anna wrote about him in a recent letter."

Daniel tried unsuccessfully to force his index finger into the tiny handle of the cup. He estimated that he would need eight refills to equal a proper mug of coffee. "Did you know Birk is here in Lillesand?" He felt a sharp pain in his thigh at the same time he heard Ingrid cough. "He wants to develop the island property."

"Oh yes!" Marta refilled the coffee cups, and passed the waffles again. "Anna is so proud of him. She thinks it is wonderful that he is finally showing some interest in his heritage. Of course, Anna is no longer in a position to manage the family property. Naturally, she is glad that he is taking on the responsibility."

Daniel lost interest in the coffee and waffle. In the edge of his vision, he could see that Ingrid was looking closely at him, and it made him nervous. He cleared his throat. "Did she turn over her rights to the property to Birk? I mean legally."

"Oh, I do not know anything about that, but I would think

she would be happy to let Birk have full control over the property. More coffee?"

"Did Anna ever mention me?"

Marta frowned, and seemed to look for the answer on the ceiling for several seconds. "Yes, it was you . . . your family . . ." She sighed. "Anna never did get over that. She had regrets." She sighed again. "Forgive me; would either of you like strawberries on your waffles?" Marta giggled. "Well, that was silly of me. I intended to buy strawberries, but . . ."

Daniel felt Ingrid's hand on his back, and he half listened as Ingrid steered the conversation to Marta's garden. Their conversation became a distant hum. He wondered if Marta had all the information. Was it possible that Birk was manipulating Anna? He reviewed what Marta had said, and could find no support for his theory. Ingrid was playing with the end of her braid, and he knew that he had to rescue her. Just as Marta started to identify each piece of her porcelain collection, Daniel made a show of looking at his watch. "Ingrid, you asked me to remind you. You have a meeting with a client at the marina in just twenty minutes."

"Oh my goodness," Ingrid said. "Time slips away so quickly when you are with good company."

Neither Ingrid nor Daniel spoke during the ride to the marina, but as soon as they exited the car, Ingrid said, "I really do have to get back to work, but I am worried about you. What are you going to do now?"

Daniel shrugged. "Walk. I think best when I walk."

"Meet me here at five. We are going to eat at The Kettle."

"You have been such a good friend Ingrid—and patient. How can I ever repay you?"

"There is something. Solveig and Sarah are coming to visit with me this weekend. Sarah has asked if she could sail with us again. You are so good with her. Will you come?"

Daniel felt an objection surface in his mind, but he quickly suppressed it. He agreed, and then set out toward the Lillesand centre. As he walked, doubts filled his mind. Of course, he thought, Birk had a right to take the cabin away. He is a member of the owner's family. Who is Daniel Nordal? A troublemaker? He could see the headline in Aftenposten: Mad Man of the Skerries Captured at Last. What was to become of him? His thoughts turned to Linda and Emma, and he reminded himself that his own life was unimportant. What counsel would Linda have given him? Linda was always wise. She loved the island, and that was enough for him.

He spent the afternoon walking, and struggling with his conflicted thoughts. Having no interest in food, he considered cancelling dinner with Ingrid.

The afternoon passed, and he found himself at The Kettle with Ingrid. The fish soup brought back his appetite, and he began to relax. Ingrid asked for his advice about a boat restoration project. He knew very well; she did not need his advice for she was one of the best boat builders in Southern Norway, but he offered an obvious suggestion to further the conversation.

"You would be so good at the marina," Ingrid said. "You are a talented woodworker. What are you doing with your skills?"

I see it now. First Solveig with her project, and then Ingrid with this. If Daniel has work, he will forget about the island. "They say a boat builder is a carpenter that cannot work with a straight line." He waited for a laugh or a comeback, but her face revealed no reaction.

Ingrid leaned forward. "Can we be serious?" Just then, their server came to their table with steaming plates of halibut in cream sauce, and generous portions of carrots and boiled new potatoes.

As Daniel started to eat, he realized how hungry he was. He lost himself in the meal and did not emerge until the plate was nearly empty. "We should do this more often," Daniel said as he forked the last bit of fish on his plate. "This is the best food in Lillesand."

"Yes, and the best conversation," Ingrid said flatly.

Daniel looked at his watch. "They have a wonderful apple cake, but, if I do not get going, I will be on the water after dark."

"Relax, even if you leave now the sun will set before you

get to the island. You can sleep on my boat tonight. So it is settled; we will have the cake."

They ordered coffee and cake, and Ingrid started to play with the end of her braid. "Something is bothering you," Daniel said.

She gave Daniel a weak smile and let go of her braid. "Yes, that is an understatement."

"I am sorry Ingrid, but I cannot see myself working at the marina."

Ingrid shook her head. "I gave that up between the fish soup and the halibut. But, I was thinking about what Marta said today; about Anna being pleased with Birk. Do you still think there is a need for you to defend Anna's interests? You must have been thinking about this today."

"It is not only about Anna Olsen."

"Yes, I understand that. Maybe there is another way now to close this matter. I think perhaps you could leave the island without turning your back on the past." A young woman brought them two cups of coffee and two slabs of apple cake. Daniel reached at once for his fork, but Ingrid put her hand on his. "Please wait. There is more I want to say." Daniel nodded.

"What about some kind of permanent memorial on the island?" Ingrid asked. "At the cove. A brass plaque, or something in granite, or maybe a flagpole?"

"Birk would not have it."

Ingrid released his hand. "How would you know if you do not ask him? I do not believe anyone could be so cold-hearted. It would probably suit Birk, to find a peaceful way out of this conflict with you. Maybe Eric could suggest it. What do you think?"

"I have met many people like Birk in my life. You cannot let people like that win."

Ingrid slapped both of her hands on the table. "Yes, of course. You have to win. That is the way it is—yes? Daniel has to slay the dragon at any cost." Ingrid stood. "You can have my cake too." She threw a wad of money on the table, and left the dining room.

"You do not understand. You were not there," Daniel said to the empty chair.

Daniel woke before sunrise in one of the rooms at The Kettle. He was in a foul mood. The evening had ended badly, and now there was the unanticipated expense of a room. It seemed as if a fog bank had closed in on his mind. His thoughts drifted without direction, until they ran aground. Then he would push off on a new course with an equally barren outcome. There was only one thing to do. He had to walk, and the best place to walk was the island. Just before dawn, Daniel left the room at The Kettle, and walked to his boat as fast as his legs would move.

When the island came into view, Daniel could feel the accumulated tension drain from his body. He looked forward to the familiar trails, to the smell of the pines, and to the coffee that only he knew how to make. For just a little while, he wanted to forget that Birk existed, and to take up again his comforting routine.

When he came close to the island, Daniel saw an unfamiliar boat tied to the dock. It was an open boat with a double prow, and high gunwales. A wooden boat, with clean traditional lines. The summer season brought a myriad of boats upon the water, and it was common for their owners to explore the skerries. Daniel had encountered many such boaters at the island, so he was unconcerned.

Daniel secured his craft, and saw a young man race down the bluff toward the dock. The youth appeared to Daniel to be in his early twenties, with an athletic build, and a cap of unruly blond hair. Daniel assumed that the youth did not know the island had an occupant until he saw the cabin. Now he would be anxious with Daniel's arrival. He decided to invite the young man for coffee.

The stranger came to the dock, and Daniel wished him a good morning, but the young man just stared at him. Perplexed, Daniel repeated the greeting, and extended his hand.

"I am Sondre Andersen," the young man said. He hesitated, and then reluctantly accepted Daniel's hand. "Can I help you?"

"There is nothing you can do for me." Daniel turned to examine the boat. "That is a fine boat you have. A beautiful example of traditional construction."

Sondre cocked his head to one side and a furrow appeared on his brow. "My uncle left this boat to me." He looked from Daniel to the boat. "The boat? Oh, I see!" Sondre smiled. "That is why you stopped here. Look it over if you wish."

Daniel shook his head. "No, I did not stop to see the boat. This is my destination."

Sondre's smile disappeared. "Who are you?"

"My name is Daniel Nordal, and I live in the cabin up there." He nodded toward the top of the bluff.

"You are not supposed to be here."

"I think I understand now. You are here to occupy the cabin and keep me away?"

"Well, according to—"

"Would you like some coffee?" Daniel started for the cabin; he could hear Sondre trudging behind him.

Daniel found that most of his belongings were now in the bedroom. A sleeping bag was on the sofa, and a backpack hung from a hook on the wall. The coffee beans were where he left them, so he set about to count beans into the mill. "Are you having coffee with me?"

"Mr. Nordal, I have to tell you—"

"Yes, I am certain that you do. I know you are just doing your job, and I am just making coffee. Would you put some water in that small pot and light a flame under it?" He dropped the beans into the mill. "There is enough here for both of us." He gripped the handle of the mill and swung it around. "Nothing smells better then fresh ground coffee."

Sondre pumped some water into a blackened pot, set it on the stove, and lit the burner. "I should not be doing this."

"Birk told you not to have coffee?" He pulled the tray of ground coffee from the mill and held it to his nose. "That was not fair of me. I know what you mean."

"Please, this is not personal Mr. Nordal."

"No, of course it would not be for you, but it is very personal for me."

"This is just a job—to make a little money for the summer."

"Are you a student?" Sondre nodded. "Of course. A little cabin in the skerries. A place to invite your friends. You are lucky to find such pleasant work." He dumped the ground coffee into the water. "Some people think that coffee should not be boiled, but boiling gives it character."

"What do you plan to do?" Sondre asked.

"The first thing to do is to have coffee." Daniel shrugged.

"Mr. Olsen will be here today."

"Well then, he must see that you are doing a good job." Daniel took two mugs from hooks and placed them on the counter. The coffee swirled up to the rim of the pot, and Daniel reduced the flame. After a few minutes, he filled the mugs. "Give the grinds a few minutes to settle, and develop the flavour. While we wait, let us sit and talk about our problem." They sat across from each other. Daniel studied his coffee, while Sondre pushed his mug from hand to hand. "First, I think you should be able to do your job."

The furrow left Sondre's forehead. "You are leaving then?"

"No, but you should use the cabin." Daniel took a careful sip of the coffee and grunted his approval.

"If you are not leaving—"

"Summer is almost upon us, and there is a fine spot in the middle of the island to hang a tarp. You know, I have not camped in years. I think it will be a nice change."

"But, Mr. Olsen—"

"You do not have to worry about Birk. What I choose to do is legal, and I do not care if he knows. You can tell him if you like, but he seems like a nervous person. For your peace, maybe we should keep it a secret."

While he sipped coffee, Daniel made a plan. He would take what supplies and clothes he needed to his boat. Then he would take the boat to an inlet on the far side of the island, and he would carry his supplies to the campsite. Everything hidden from the sea and from the trail.

Sondre took his first sip of coffee, and his eyes opened wide. He stood, raced for the door, and spit a stream of black fluid onto the ground. Just a kid, Daniel thought.

10

In a wooded hollow, on the windward side of the island, Daniel Nordal sat by a fire, watched his coffee boil, and reflected on the days he had camped. Birk had been to the island, and Daniel watched him, but he remained unseen. He was pleased with his decision to camp—it was satisfying for him to fool Birk. Leaving the cabin was a minor setback. Sondre was only there for the summer, and Birk could easily tire of this project. Yes, there was always a chance of winning. In the short term, it was sufficient that the island remain undeveloped. He would do what was necessary.

He heard a disturbance in the brush, so he stood slowly, and cupped his hands behind his ears. It must be a person, he concluded, for there are no large animals on the island. Then the sound of footfalls came close, and he assumed that Sondre had talked to Birk about him. Suddenly, Ingrid entered the clearing followed by Sondre. "What a tracker you are. Come, both of you. There is enough coffee for everyone."

She faced him with her hands on her hips. "You have no idea why I came here, do you?"

"How did you find me?"

Sondre backed toward the edge of the clearing. "She was going to notify the police. I had to tell her you were on the island. She was here yesterday too," Sondre said in a weak voice.

"Today is Sunday. Does that mean anything to you? Your promise?" She glared at him and waited for an answer. "Solveig and Sarah?"

"Oh my God! Are they waiting in Lillesand? I will come right now." He looked from Ingrid to Sondre then back again to Ingrid. "Sondre did not know my location. How did you find me?" He could see at the edge of his vision, Sondre making a gesture of holding a coffee cup and holding his nose.

Daniel laughed. "Of course, you followed the smell of my coffee. I bet they can smell it in Lillesand."

"How can you laugh?" Ingrid asked. "You were gone, and the boat was gone. There is a stranger in the cabin, and he says he does not know you. And yesterday, I had to leave my guests alone and spend the day searching for you. You make me so mad." Ingrid covered her face with her hands and shook her head. After a long silence, she removed her hands and revealed wet eyes. "Look at you! Now you live in the woods like an animal because of this obsession of yours."

Sondre turned, and like a cat stalking a bird, stepped lightly from the clearing.

"Sarah had her heart set on sailing with us, but mostly she

wanted a lesson from you. Solveig said that Sarah would only agree to come because you would be there. You have no idea how disappointed she is. There is still time if you hurry, but after today, I do not care if I ever see you again." Ingrid wiped her eyes with her sleeve.

Daniel moaned and poured his coffee over the fire. "I am sorry Ingrid. I am so sorry." He started to kick dirt on the fire. "I will make it up to Sarah and to you. My boat is close; it will be the fastest way back to the dock." Without talking further, they took Daniel's boat to the dock, where Ingrid took his boat in tow to Lillesand.

They joined Solveig and Sarah at Ingrid's apartment where Daniel apologized repeatedly. Sarah expressed relief that she was spared from another boring day, and Solveig withheld her customary hug.

When they assembled on Ingrid's sloop, Sarah begged to steer again. Daniel offered to work with her, and tend the mainsail. Ingrid said she would tend the jib sheets, and asked Solveig to join her. The two women plunged immediately into whispered conversation.

Once they were sufficiently clear of land, Daniel worked with Sarah on turning through the wind. At Daniel's prompting, Sarah called out "prepare to come about," but Ingrid was too deep in conversation to hear. It took some good-natured shouting from Daniel about the incompetence of the crew to get her attention. After a short time, Sarah gave warning again with the same results. At the fourth attempt, the shouting ceased to be good-natured, and Daniel gave up on the exercise.

When they cleared the harbour, Daniel decided to teach Sarah about steering by the compass. In only five minutes, Sarah had learned to use a compass heading as her guide. "Look behind the boat," Daniel said. "Have we been going in a straight line?"

She looked back at the twisting wake. "Am I doing that?"

"With each wave, you feel the wheel push against your hands. Yes?" She nodded. "And you push back. Try not to push back so hard. Push just enough to keep the wave from turning the boat. The compass can help you learn this Sarah. See how the card rotates with each wave? You want to keep the card steady. There, that is the way. After awhile, you will see there is a rhythm to this, and you will not need to watch the compass so closely."

Daniel watched Sarah's intense focus on the compass. Slowly her expression melted into a broad smile. Her apparent joy at mastering this challenge, reminded him of when he first learned to sail. When had he last felt that kind of joy? "You are doing well Sarah. Better than me at your age."

Sarah looked back at the nearly straight wake and squealed for Solveig to look. Solveig moved to the stern, and in spite of her ignorance of seamanship, gushed words of admiration.

"You are very patient with her," Solveig said in Norwegian.

"Now that we have the crew's attention," Daniel said while looking at Ingrid, "we should change course before we come aground on the island off the port bow."

"I think this would be a good time for Sarah to learn to handle the jib sheets," Ingrid said. So Sarah moved forward with Ingrid, and Daniel took the wheel. Daniel offered the wheel to Solveig, but she acted as if he had offered her a poisonous serpent.

After many course changes, Sarah could handle the jib without assistance. The frequent turning was draining the colour from Solveig's face. Because he was close to her, Daniel decided that it would be wise to stop the manoeuvres. "Send Sarah back to me again," he said.

Ingrid hesitated, and then said, "I want to go over the fine points of trimming the jib with her."

"I think she will need more time at the helm first. Let her come back."

"No, she will stay here," Ingrid, said in Norwegian.

Daniel wondered about Ingrid's insistence until Solveig said in a whisper, "we need to talk." She cleared her throat. "Yes, for Sarah's sake, we need to talk in Norwegian for now. I want to be frank with you, and I hope you are not offended." Solveig sighed. "When I see you helping Sarah, you remind me of the Daniel I used to know. What has happened to you? Yes, I know you have had difficulties. I do not want to be insensitive, but everyone has had difficulties in their life. You have a very good friend in Ingrid, but you are pushing her away at every turn. Maybe she is more than a good friend. Do you want to lose her support? And, forgive me Daniel, you are acting like a fool."

"But, I cannot abandon—"

"Abandon what? You cannot abandon what no longer exists."

"What I have in my heart exists." He shifted in his seat. "Why do you want me to be something different?"

"Look at how you are living. Hiding on an island like a fugitive. I know you have always been a loner, but this . . ." She observed Sarah looking at her, and forced a smile. "I worry about you Daniel; Ingrid worries about you too."

"There is no need to worry, but I need advice about—"

"Yes, about Birk Olsen. Ingrid has told me about your visit to her sister. Accept what is. Birk is a member of the family that owns the island, and you have nothing in writing."

Daniel's knuckles turned white against the wheel. "Maybe there is something written somewhere. Maybe Birk knows this, but he is trying to take advantage of Anna and me."

Solveig gave a sigh that caused Ingrid and Sarah to turn. "Where do you get such an idea?" She scanned the clouds. "If you believe this, get a lawyer. There is nothing more I can tell you."

Daniel shook his head. "I could not afford a lawyer."

"I can help you."

"What? But, you do not believe . . ."

"It does not matter what I believe."

"Oh no, I could never accept money from you."

"I have an idea that will help us both."

Daniel pushed Solveig's proposal from his mind. During the previous twenty-four hours, he had thought of little else, but he became weary. The reasons he found for accepting the proposal, were no stronger than the reasons for rejecting it. There was nothing gained by continuing to struggle with the choices.

Daniel did what he always did, when the fog bank closed on his mind; he walked. Setting out to circle the island, he exchanged greetings with Sondre as if they had been good neighbours for years. One loop of the island became two, then three, and then he stopped counting. In the end, he gained no insight, but discovered that he was hungry.

At his campsite, he opened two tins of mackerel in tomato sauce, and a package of flatbread. After consuming the food, he sat against a boulder where a blanket of drowsiness rose over him. Just as he was about to surrender consciousness, he heard the unmistakable sound of Eric's launch.

He climbed over the rocky, trackless spine of the island to a place where he could observe the cove. His vantage point was a flat rock where he could lie and look down toward the shore. The cove, he decided, was where he would draw the line.

The rock was warm from the sun, and Daniel had to fight to stay awake. His thoughts turned to Sarah, and he thought of her enthusiasm for adventure. She reminded him of Emma. How old would Emma be? He thought for a minute. Twelve—almost a young woman. What would she be like now? She would want to be with her friends on Long Island; she would no longer want to visit Norway. Of course, there would be no one her age to talk with on the island. Maybe they would just fight. The thought depressed him, so he went back in his mind to when Linda and Emma were alive. In his mind, nothing had changed. Linda was sitting there, with his head cradled in her lap. "What am I going to do?" he asked her softly. Her answer was in a language he could not understand, but it was comforting to hear her voice.

Daniel climbed from sleep, aware only of the hard surface beneath him. He lifted his head from a puddle of drool that streaked his face with dirt, and looked around. Awareness came quickly when he saw the cove. His muscles ached, and the glare from the water hurt his eyes. Was Birk still on the island? Had he been to the cove? Why could he not stay awake?

He slid down the bank to the cove, and examined the ground. There was a disposable cigarette lighter, but it could have been there for days. Footprints crossed the sand, but Daniel could not tell if they were fresh. He took a stick and marked out the footprints so he would be able to tell which were new in the future. When he finished, he collapsed onto the bench with a groan.

Ingrid's words came to him; "Now you live in the woods like an animal." What was he doing? He was a grown man hiding in the woods, and creeping over rocks; spying on another man, and looking at footprints like a trapper. Daniel looked at his clothes; they were torn and filthy from pushing through the brush and sliding down the bank. Then he imagined himself walking out into the water and letting the current take him. The sea that took the best of his life could have the rest of it now. Maybe that was the only way. Let the devil take the island. He pushed himself to his feet and took a deep breath.

Then, in his mind, he saw cottages, and children playing by the water. A little girl ran into the water, and swam a short distance. That girl started to thrash about and she screamed, and screamed, and screamed. The other children ran to Daniel and looked up at him with pleading eyes. He heard his own voice yell, "No this cannot happen," and the image of the children disappeared. He slammed his fists, and kicked at the bench. *No this cannot happen! The hell with a plan. The hell with Birk.* Why should he care about legal rights? What could Birk do to a man that was already dead? He would argue with

Birk until the man could no longer stand to listen to him. Yes, Birk would hear him loud and clear. He could not move fast enough—he headed at once to the cabin.

The shut cabin door did not slow Daniel down. He put his weight to it, and drove the door open. In a few seconds, he scanned the two rooms, and found them empty except for Sondre's belongings, which were scattered everywhere. Daniel called, but heard only his own voice resonate from the walls. Then he rushed to the dock, and saw Sondre sitting there reading a book.

When Sondre saw Daniel, he smiled and waved. "Ah here is the ghost of No-Name Island. I hope I did not make trouble for you with your lady friend."

"Was Birk here today?"

"Sure, you dodged him again." Sondre looked carefully at Daniel. "Did you fall?"

"I must talk with him," Daniel said firmly.

"Well, you missed him. But, he said he would be back at least one more time. After that, you will not have to worry for the summer. You can stay in the open, and it will not matter."

"What has happened?"

"Can't spend my life in this damn country," Sondre said in English, mimicking Birk. "This place had better pay off for my time and effort. The only one making money is my lawyer."

"No, he gave up?"

"Oh no, not yet," Sondre said, reverting to Norwegian. "It seems there are too many legal delays for his liking. He is impatient; everything is taking longer, and costing more than he expected. And, he has talked about big deals waiting for him at home."

"And, he can leave without worry, now that he thinks I have been scared away by you," Daniel added. "When is he coming back?"

Sondre shrugged. "His plane leaves on Friday from Oslo. He could stop by any time before then."

"He will probably need to leave Lillesand on Thursday, so I will guess he will be here by Wednesday. When will he come back to Norway?"

"He said he would contact me before I return to school. Is something wrong?"

"I came here now to confront . . . but, never mind. Everything has changed. So much to think about. Someone made a proposal that maybe I should consider."

11

Daniel spent the night resting on a bed of moss, looking at the slow progression of the stars across the pine boughs, and trying to reach a decision. By the time the morning haze erased the stars, he felt at peace, and he made a choice. For the first time in many weeks, Daniel felt energized. The first thing he thought to do would be to share the news with Ingrid. She would be pleased, and perhaps his decision would heal the strain that had come between them. Knudsen's bakery would be the place to meet her before she went to the marina, and he had just enough time to get there when it opened.

Greta brought Daniel coffee and a raisin roll, and a warning not to make a mess. It was comforting to come back to a taste of his former routine, and to have Greta fuss at him. He had picked out half of the raisins from the roll, when Ingrid came through the door. She glanced at him, then looked away and walked to the counter where she ordered a coffee to go. As she turned to leave, Daniel left his table and walked up to her.

"Ingrid, do you have just a minute?"

"No."

"I have some news that I think you will want to hear."

"I have had all the news I can handle." She walked toward him. "Excuse me, I have to go." She continued to walk, with Daniel walking backwards in front of her.

"This is different."

She stopped walking. "Is it about the island or Birk?"

"Well yes, but—"

"I have to get to work. Excuse me." She brushed past Daniel and strode from the bakery.

Daniel stood alone for a moment in the doorway, and then he started after her. He heard Greta call to him, but it was unclear what she wanted. With long strides, he reached Ingrid quickly. "Please, just listen. Only one minute."

Ingrid did not look at him or change her stride. "I think you should go back and pay Greta."

"I am leaving the island."

Ingrid stopped abruptly, and some of her coffee spilled onto the sidewalk. "What did you say?"

He told her again, and she threw her free arm around his neck and gave him a hug. "Daniel, I am so happy for you." She stepped back and smiled broadly. "You did not finish your coffee. Come back to Knudsen's and tell me all about it." She took his arm and they walked together back to the bakery. Daniel had expected her to be pleased, but the intensity of her reaction unsettled him.

Greta was cleaning up the raisin pile when Daniel walked in. "Only one mess a day from you. That is all I allow," Greta said. When she saw Ingrid follow, her scowl turned to a grin. Immediately she brought two fresh mugs of coffee and a plate of raison rolls.

As soon as they sat, Ingrid reached across the table and grabbed his hands. "Go on, tell me about it."

"You will be pleased to hear that I have accepted Solveig's offer."

She leaned back, and her smile waned. "What offer?"

"I will do the carpentry work for her shop in Lyngør this summer."

"There is carpentry work available in Lillesand. Why go so far? Oh, I see—another island."

Daniel sighed. "I thought you would be pleased. Solveig is a friend of ours."

"Of course; I am too hard on you. There are people living there. It is good that you will not be isolated." She forced the corners of her mouth up about a centimetre. "I am happy for you Daniel. What made you decide to do this?"

Daniel repeated what Sondre told him. "You seem upset."

"No, why do you say that?"

"You are twisting your braid."

"I should cut this off." She brought the end of the braid to her cheek. "Perhaps I was hoping for something different but this is a good thing. Yes, you will have a summer away, and maybe you will have a fresh outlook in the end."

"The money from this job will pay for a lawyer if I need one, but in the mean time, Birk is away. Maybe he will lose interest." He started to pull raisins from the roll. "I plan to call Solveig today about my decision. Maybe I can start next week."

"I should have known, but, it is a change." She lined up the raisins that Daniel discarded. "Of course, I will drive you to the ferry at Gjeving when you are ready to go. Oh my God, I am playing with raisins now."

"Thank you, but I will not need a ride." His face brightened. "I am going to take my boat."

Ingrid's mouth fell open. "You do not want to take a trip like that in an open boat. If you go on the weekend, I will tow it for you."

Daniel shook his head. "I will be fine."

Solveig expressed delight when Daniel told her he had accepted the job. She would be at Lyngør on the weekend, but he could come early if he chose. The door was unlocked.

Daniel planned to leave at first light the next day. He did not have a nautical chart, but would rely instead on a road map that gave details of the coast. It would be a simple matter of following the coast, he reasoned.

After cleaning up his campsite, he loaded his belongings

into the boat and motored to the island's dock. With Sondre's help, he unloaded items he did not need for the trip, and moved them into the bedroom. With the exception of the toolbox in the bedroom closet, he had everything in the boat he would need. Because it would be his last night on the island for many weeks, he decided that he would spend the rest of the day at the cove. When night came, he would return to the dock, and sleep on his boat.

A wave of sadness came over Daniel as he surveyed the cove. He had a sense that he was saying goodbye to a vital part of his life. Unexpected doubts filled his mind. Was his decision the right one? He found a temporary diversion in cleaning up the bits of twigs and tangled fishing line that had washed onto the rocks and sand. When there was no more work to do, he sat on the bench, and reminded himself that leaving was temporary and necessary. Still, he had a suspicion that the scene he was looking at would be changed forever if he left. He closed his eyes, and dwelt on his doubts until he became lost in misery. It was not until the sun dropped to the horizon did he climb from despair, and with a sense of surrender Daniel realized he would have to leave. It was time to retrieve his toolbox and prepare the boat for sleeping.

On the way to the cabin, he heard the sound of Eric's launch approach the island. Birk would certainly see his boat, and he smiled when he imagined Birk's response. Shortly after the launch's engine became still, he heard raised voices from the cabin. As he came closer, he heard Sondre say, "He is just visiting the cove."

Daniel looked forward to confronting Birk, and quickened his pace. But, as he walked, he realized that conflict with Birk on the eve of his departure would endanger his plan. Maybe Birk would not be so confident about leaving Norway. Daniel would announce that he was leaving the island, but he would not speak directly to Birk. He would speak only to Sondre and Eric, and he would speak only Norwegian.

He arrived at the cabin, entered, and wished everyone a good evening in Norwegian.

"What are you doing here?" Birk asked.

"I still need to transfer my toolbox."

"Speak English!"

Eric crossed the room to Daniel. "Are you going away?"

Birk crossed his arms and scowled. "What's everybody saying?"

"You can tell Birk that I am moving away from here."

Eric relayed the message, and asked, "Where are you going?"

"This is just between us Eric. I am going to Lyngør. My boat is packed, and I will leave in the morning."

"In that boat? Alone? Have you made such a trip before? Do you have a chart?"

Daniel shook his head, and went to the bedroom to get his toolbox.

"Your summer should be calm with him out of the way," Birk said to Sondre. "How did you scare him off?"

"Tell him we wrestled for the cabin and I lost," Daniel said from the bedroom.

"It is his idea to go," Sondre said in English.

With toolbox in hand, Daniel passed through the main room and said goodbye. The last voice he heard was Birk asking, "What did he say?" There was no answer.

The boat was overcrowded, Daniel decided. There were expendable items he would place in a pile on the dock, and then move them to the cabin after Birk and Eric left. Winter clothes were the first to go. The daggerboard was unnecessary because he would only use the motor. The mainsail, furled on the boom, was not in the way—he would leave it there. Oars were cumbersome, but one never knew when an emergency might arise. Next was the canned food. He could eat in any one of the many communities along his route.

Eric came alone to the dock, and climbed aboard his launch. After a few minutes, he hopped down to the dock with a sheet of paper in his hands, and approached Daniel. "You have never made the trip to Lyngør," Eric said, "so I want you to have this." He handed the paper to Daniel, who recognized it as a nautical chart. "It is too easy to become disoriented in the skerries. You must be able to know where you are at all times. Do you have a compass?"

"As long as the sun shines, I will know my direction, and besides, I will always be in sight of land."

"You should not do this Daniel." Eric shook his head. "I know you are a stubborn man, so I will not try to argue with you." He extended his hand. "Good luck to you."

Birk came down the trail whistling, and called out, "hoist anchor."

Daniel laughed. "Does he know what an anchor is, and that you are not using one?"

"The forecast predicts high winds along the coast tomorrow afternoon. Be careful."

"I will be safe at Lyngør by afternoon."

The roar of the motor woke Sondre, who stumbled to the dock to wish Daniel well. Daniel was tempted to go to the cabin to make coffee, but decided he would wait until the first mainland village where he would have breakfast as well. That morning he felt comfortable about his decision, and he looked forward to the trip.

With the help of Eric's chart, he identified Skauerøya and followed its coast looking for Saltholmen Light. When he finally passed the lighthouse, the sun was high in the eastern sky. He expected that he would have been there much earlier, but he had never come this way before. Even if the trip takes several days, it will not be a problem, he decided. He proceeded southeast to skirt the finger of mainland east of Lillesand, but it seemed as if the boat were moving in slow motion. Landmarks he saw an hour earlier were still close to where they were then. Aware that it was unreliable to judge speed by distant landmarks, he pushed the matter from his mind.

Heat from the sun, the constant whine of the motor, and lack of food and coffee, caused Daniel to feel irritable. He started to obsess about strong coffee and raisin rolls. There was a flask of drinking water, but soon it was empty, and Daniel started to worry.

Daniel checked the gasoline level, and was surprised to find that his fuel consumption was higher than expected. He would need to come ashore soon, and if he expected to make any progress, he would need to buy an extra gas can. Relying on stopping points for food and water had become another obvious mistake.

After an anxious hour, Daniel spotted a cluster of buildings on shore. If he went closer to inspect, he would burn more fuel. He decided to take a chance, so he swung the bow to point at a Norwegian flag flying near the buildings. The buildings were curiously uniform, and then he could see rows of camping trailers, and a minute later, tents at the tree line. Splendid, a campground, he concluded. There will be a market, and there will be fuel for sale.

Because there was no longer a need to monitor fuel consumption, and he did not want to waste time, he opened the throttle as far as he could. The bow rose at once, the wind whipped his body and refreshed him, and his mind turned again to coffee and raisin rolls. As he came closer to the campground, he could make out a dock and a row of small boats.

He knew that the heavy boat would slow abruptly once he cut power, so he decided to come to about 200 yards from the dock at full power. He was wasting too much time. Daniel had no doubt now; he would need several days to reach Lyngør. His hand tensed on the throttle as the dock rushed closer. When he judged the distance to be right, he twisted the throttle. The motor continued to scream. He twisted harder. The dock raced closer. People ran from the dock. He pushed the tiller hard to port, and the boat banked sharply to starboard. The boat's momentum caused it to slip on its beam. The port side slammed into and rode shrieking up against a piling. Water spilled over the gunwale. The motor, still screaming, pushed the boat toward open water.

Daniel reached under the motor cowling and found the fuel stopcock. It was stiff, but he put all his effort into closing the fuel line. The engine died abruptly, and in seconds, the boat was bobbing on the swells. He leaned over the port side, and explored the hull with his hands. To his relief there were no broken boards. There were three inches of water aboard, but it was not a threat. The motor was his primary worry; he would have to use the stopcock to regulate speed.

He looked back at the campground, and saw a large group

of people gathering by the dock. It would be best, he decided, to find another source of food and fuel, and going back to Lillesand was not an option.

Daniel followed a northeast course along the mainland coast. There were scattered buildings, but no communities that he could see from the water. Thirst had become oppressive; an obsession for water replaced the one for coffee and raisin rolls. An hour from the campground, he decided that any dwelling would do. He must have water. Then he spotted a cottage with a car. Someone was at home, so he pointed the bow to shore and opened the fuel stopcock wider. Just as the bow turned, the engine sputtered and died. As the boat lost way, two-foot swells turned the boat so that it caught the waves broadside. Daniel knew at once; he had pushed his luck too far—the fuel was gone.

With the tiller, Daniel managed to regain some control of the boat's heading, but the boat was drifting away from the coast. He set the oars, and began to pull. After a dozen strokes, he stopped and used his inhaler. It became obvious that his only option was to use the sails. Without a daggerboard, it would have to be a minimum amount of canvas.

He unfurled the mainsail, and gave it enough line, so that it spilled most of its air. Just enough for control and forward motion, he reasoned. The boat slipped on its beam, almost as much as it went forward. With each gust of wind, the boat heeled to its gunwale.

Clouds scudded across the sky, and blocked the sun, and the wind whipped the sea into three-foot swells; the boat heeled to where it started to take on water. He judged that trying to come ashore in a poorly controlled boat in rising seas was more dangerous than staying offshore. The boat was taking on too much water; the mainsail would not do, he would have to use the jib. He turned the mainsail loose so that it snapped impotently in the wind. The boat has a lee helm, he remembered, maybe he could turn that flaw to his advantage.

He turned the tiller loose and crawled forward. There seemed to be no choice, the oars were in the way; he threw them into the sea. Daniel pulled the jib from the forward locker, and attached it to the forestay. It took several minutes to rig the jib in the tossing boat. Hand over hand he took in just enough of the starboard jib sheet until he could see a wake at the stern. Yes, this boat will sail downwind without a hand on the tiller, he exulted, just what I needed. Satisfied that the boat sailed better with the jib, he positioned himself at the stern. All he needed to do now was furl the mainsail before it snapped itself to shreds. He rose up from the seat to stretch forward to the mast. At that moment, a gust of wind caught the mainsail and brought its boom violently across the stern. The last thing Daniel saw was the boat sailing away from him—downwind.

12

"Mr. Nordal, Mr. Nordal," a woman's voice persisted.

Daniel was at peace, and he chose not to be disturbed. Neither the voice nor the shaking of his arm would cause him to yield.

"He should have come out by now," a second female voice said. "An hour since we stopped the drip."

"I have a few calls to make," the first voice said. "Page me if he comes around, but I should be back in twenty minutes."

Yes, come back another time. Daniel drifted—sometimes aware of drifting, and sometimes not. Then he became aware of pressure on his side. Or, was it in his side? And it became painful. Then, he heard a piercing screech. *Shut the clock off. It cannot be morning already.* "Karen, will you hit the reset for me," someone far, far, away called. Fire consumed Daniel's side, and he struggled to escape. He opened his mouth and yelled for help, but only a weak squeak reached his ears. It worked; people were coming. Fuzzy, out of focus people. His hand went to the fire. "Do not pull on that Mr. Nordal." Someone clutched his wrist and yanked his hand from the fire.

Daniel could not comprehend why they ignored the fire and chose to ask silly questions. Of course, he knew who the prime minister was, and of course, he knew what year it was. Enough of that. If they would stop the burning, he could just slip away again.

"The nurse is getting something to make you feel more comfortable," a female voice said. "Mr. Nordal, I am Dr. Halvorsen, and you are in the Arendal hospital."

The truth came to Daniel at once. "The boat," he said hoarsely.

"You remember—a good sign. There was trauma to your chest—"

"The boom. The boom came across . . ."

Dr. Halvorsen nodded slowly. "Of course; that explains it." She told Daniel that he had been in the hospital for three weeks. The boom fractured four of his ribs, one of which had penetrated his right lung. There was a tube in his side, which would have to stay a little longer, and until that morning, a machine helped him breathe. Someone called the rescue service, when his boat came ashore. While Dr. Halvorsen spoke, Daniel watched a nurse inject something into the tube that entered his arm. It was fortunate, she assured him, that he had worn a life jacket. Still, he had aspirated seawater, and that had complicated the management of his trauma. She knew about his asthma—the inhaler was with him when he came to the trauma centre, and she had checked with the

Lillesand clinic. Daniel felt the burning in his side fade, and he was having trouble keeping his eyes open.

"There is someone . . . a woman who has come here every day," Dr. Halvorsen said. "This is not a good time for a visitor, but maybe just for a minute if you wish." Daniel grunted an approximation of "yes," and Dr. Halvorsen nodded to the nurse.

Though he had assumed correctly that the woman was Ingrid, the woman that approached his bed was in some way a stranger. She lacked Ingrid's purposeful stride, and clear gaze. The woman approached hesitantly, and he could see that her crimson streaked eyes avoided looking directly at him. *Have I done this to her?* She grasped his hand in her own, and then she slowly turned her gaze to his face.

"I will never forgive myself," Ingrid said in a soft voice. "This is my fault. I am so sorry."

Daniel struggled to raise his head. "How can that be? It is only my stubbornness."

"Please, lie back. The boat . . . it was flawed . . . that is my fault. I should not have sold it. Can you forgive me?"

Daniel shook his head. "No, the boat saved my life. Because it ran downwind it went ashore and attracted attention." He coughed. "I was unconscious in the water." Daniel examined her face for acknowledgment, but found no sign. "Any other boat would have come about and drifted seaward." He cleared his throat. "Can you see that?" A whine came from somewhere over his head; a nurse came and silenced it.

"I think that is enough talking," the nurse said. She looked at Ingrid. "You can return later if you wish, but Mr. Nordal needs to rest now."

Daniel started to squeeze Ingrid's hand, to reassure her, but her hand slipped away. He turned his head and, fighting the heaviness of his eyes, watched her walk away, but before she had gone far, his eyes prevailed.

Daniel remained in the intensive care unit for another week, and Ingrid continued to visit. More than his physical pain, Daniel ached when he saw the suffering in Ingrid's eyes. Later, in the surgical ward, Eric came to visit, and Daniel spoke of Ingrid's anguish. "You are right, of course," Eric said. "The lee helm had nothing to do with your situation." Eric smiled. "It has everything to do with a stubborn man. Perhaps she will listen to me."

"Tell me Eric . . . I did not want to ask Ingrid . . . my boat?"

Eric rubbed his chin. "I have not seen the site, but I have been told. The coast is rocky, and with the wind . . ."

Daniel looked away. "I see. The lee helm that saved me, destroyed my boat."

Eric nodded. "I will speak with Ingrid."

Two days after Eric's visit, Ingrid came with Solveig to the hospital. Daniel tried to apologize to Solveig for not being able to work on her shop, but she dismissed his attempts as nonsense. "The shop will not open for another year," Solveig said. "If you still want the job after you recover, I would welcome it." She wagged a finger at him. "Do not even think about it until then."

Beleaguered by persistent pain, and recurring shortness of breath, Daniel recovered at a disappointing pace. Just when discharge from the hospital seemed possible, pneumonia developed in his right lung that was resistant to therapy. He spent another week in intensive care, and by the time he had recovered sufficiently for discharge, it was the middle of August.

For weeks, he had struggled with the choice—should he go to Lyngør to help Solveig, or should he return to the island. In the end, he chose to keep his promise to Solveig. He could always make a day trip to Lillesand. Solveig accepted his offer on the condition that he did not start work immediately. He could come to Lyngør to rest, and plan the project. Both Ingrid and Solveig offered to drive him to the ferry at Gjeving, but Daniel insisted that he could travel without assistance.

It took two buses to get to Gjeving, and he was exhausted when he arrived. In less than ten minutes, the ferry crossed to Lyngør, and Daniel surrendered twenty-five crowns to the ferry man at the dock at Holmen.

As soon as his feet touched land, he saw Solveig rush from

The Blue Lantern. She called to him, and engulfed him in a hug. Then she pushed him away as if to examine him. She wants to see if she did any damage, Daniel guessed. "I am ready for work," Daniel said, and realized at once, how false that statement was.

Solveig sucked in a lung full of air as if she had been submerged in the Sound for several minutes. "No." She shook her head. "Never mind that. Right now, we are going to have some of the best fish soup in the world." She nodded toward the restaurant. "And then . . . you are going to have a good long rest."

"I have been resting all summer," Daniel said. Solveig dismissed his declaration with a wave of her hand, and picked up his duffle bag.

It was as if he had never tasted food before. Each spoonful of fish soup took Daniel further away from the awareness of his injuries. However, when they set out on the trail to Odden, and his rubbery legs shook, he became conscious, once again, of his limitations. Daniel made a feeble protest when Solveig insisted on carrying his bag, but he knew he would not be able to manage on his own.

They entered the ground floor sitting room that was to become Solveig's shop. On the floor along the front wall, Daniel saw a new toolbox, and a power saw. "When this project is completed, I plan to rent the upstairs apartment, but for now

135

I will stay there when I am on Lyngør." Solveig said. "Then, I will use the living space behind the shop for myself. This summer I fixed up the room in the back. That is where you can stay while you are here."

Solveig led him into a snug room that contained an upholstered chair, and an oak table with two matching chairs. Under a double window he saw a sink, and a counter-top electric stove. She opened a door that revealed a narrow bedroom with a built-in bunk. Daniel guessed that this had been a housekeeper's apartment. Perhaps the housekeeper for a prosperous shipowner from the days of sail. Solveig sucked in a deep breath. "Perhaps you should get some rest, and tonight we will have a nice meal at The Blue Lantern."

He would need the rest, he thought, if he were to take that walk again. But the lure of a good meal was sufficient for him to nod in agreement. "Are there lumber and building supply dealers on these islands?" He was sure of the answer, but Daniel wanted to see if Solveig had thought through the project.

"Of course not. When you are ready, you can make inquiries. Risør must have all that you could want. Later, we can talk about a credit account, and of course, your salary."

"It will be expensive to bring material here."

"I expect so. But enough of that—it is your first day out of the hospital. There is plenty of time." She waved her arm in an arc. "Until next spring if you choose. I know you lost your

136

tools with your boat, so I ordered what you see in the front room. You will probably need other items, and I want you to use my account."

"No! On that, I must be firm. My tools are my responsibility."

When Solveig left, Daniel sat in the upholstered chair, intending to rest for a few minutes. When he woke, the light in the room was dim, and he was unsure where he was. Gradually, he became aware that he spent the entire afternoon sleeping in the chair. In a panic, he checked his watch, and discovered it was time to join Solveig.

He walked through the cottage garden to the seawall, and looked for signs of activity. It seemed odd to him, that when he walked to the cottage with Solveig from The Blue Lantern they did not meet anyone on the path. Daniel looked across the Sound to Outer Lyngør, and surveyed the row of houses by the shore. There were scattered lights but he could see no people. So, this is what Lyngør is like when the summer season is over, Daniel reflected. The view appeared tranquil to Daniel—a very different feel from the island at Lillesand. He decided that this would be a good place to recover, and plan. Still, he felt a gnawing in his gut—he would need to return to Lillesand soon.

The weariness of walking to the restaurant, gave way to the delight Daniel experienced from his meal. He gave undivided attention to the mackerel and boiled potatoes, emerging briefly to see a satisfied smile on Solveig's lips. Later he devoured two servings of apple cake, and three refills of coffee. It was only when he finished eating, did he wonder what Solveig ate, if anything.

Solveig touched his hand. "I do hope you like the way I set up the rooms for you." As he nodded, it occurred to him that his rooms contained new bedding and towels, and undoubtedly many items he had yet to notice. "Good, good." She patted his hand.

"I would like to repay you for what you have provided . . . out of my salary."

"Nonsense. The rooms needed to be furnished." She cleared her throat. "Before your accident, you told me that you wanted to work so you could afford a lawyer. Is that still your wish?"

Daniel hesitated. "If a lawyer becomes necessary, then yes, I will need money. I still must do whatever I can."

Solveig frowned. "I see. Well, I promised to help, and I will. If you wish, I will contact the lawyer I use, and ask him what he thinks about this business. For all the money I give him, that would be a small favour. Then, we can talk about this some more."

Daniel started to talk, but Solveig cut him off. "Yes, you can accept a favour from a friend."

"I still have some money."

"We will not talk about money tonight." She insisted on paying the bill, and as they were leaving the restaurant she asked, "Would you care to join me for a glass of wine before you retire?" Daniel did not know what to say. What does she mean? Go back inside The Blue Lantern? Go to her apartment? Solveig took hold of Daniel's arm. "How thoughtless of me. Of course, you are tired and want to rest. Perhaps another time."

Daniel woke long after sunrise, and found the house to be disturbingly quiet. He felt an urgent need for coffee, so he searched the cabinets and shelves with a growing sense of panic. Solveig had stocked the apartment with a generous assortment of staples, but there was no coffee. He dressed and set out at once for Holmen, but The Blue Lantern was not open for breakfast. Daniel had no choice but to take the ferry to Gjeving.

While Daniel waited for the ferry, he decided that he must have a boat of his own. The ferry schedule would restrict him, and he would still have to walk over the trails and bridge to the cottage at Odden. There was a water taxi that could take him directly to the seawall by the cottage, but it would be too expensive to use on a regular basis. He decided that a skiff would suit him. It would have to be light and inexpensive, and that would mean fibreglass. As soon as he had breakfast, he would look for a used boat.

At the Gjeving marina, he found coffee and breakfast. He also found a greasy fibreglass skiff with oars, and an old but well maintained outboard motor. The price was reasonable, so he bought it. He purchased coffee beans, a coffee grinder, and fuel, which he loaded into the skiff. Though nervous about getting into a small boat again, he was delighted to be at the cottage in just ten minutes.

The noise of the motor brought Solveig to the seawall where Daniel explained where he had been. "How thoughtless of me," Solveig said. "Of course, you need a boat. Yes, my mind is too scattered. I will give you whatever you paid."

"The boat is my business," Daniel said curtly.

"Oh, I have offended you."

"I am sorry Solveig, but you have done too much already. A boat is something I need anyway. If I do not resell it here when I finish, maybe Ingrid will tow it back to Lillesand."

"Well, if you choose to resell it, I will buy it for the cottage." She looked at the boat and frowned. "I forgot coffee." She put her hand to her forehead. "Did you know there is a grocer directly across from here on Outer Lyngør? Just a minute away, but promise you will not row. Come, I want to show you something."

Solveig had plans for her shop spread out on the floor. She went over them with Daniel, and stressed that there was no urgency to start work. "I need to go away for awhile on business, but I want you to get all the rest you need," she said.

"My mobile number is written on a card just under the phone. Call if you have questions, or need anything." She gave him a credit card, and a generous amount of cash.

It took Daniel several days to get organized. Too much time spent, by his estimation, on the phone with building material suppliers. Locating just what he wanted and arranging for delivery consumed much of his time. It was not until the end of the first week did he feel that he was making any progress.

The island at Lillesand was always on his mind. Though he found that the project on Lyngør was satisfying, he felt guilty about being away. And he wondered if a lawyer would be of value, and if Solveig had remembered to inquire. His greatest fear was that he was wasting his time.

Daniel found pleasure in walking the island paths and trails; there was so much to explore. Occasionally he met and exchanged greetings with people, but he never engaged anyone in conversation. Ingrid phoned him a couple of times, but he heard nothing from Solveig until the end of the second week. She would arrive the following day, and she was coming for an extended visit with a couple of guests. They would all stay in the upstairs apartment and he should not trouble himself about them.

13

Daniel believed that it was the correct thing to do; he would meet Solveig and her guests at the ferry. They would have luggage to bring to the cottage, and he could help with his boat. Because Solveig never mentioned which ferry she would take, Daniel occupied much of the day meeting every ferry from Gjeving. They arrived on the last boat.

He was surprised and delighted to see Sarah hop from the boat. Then Solveig emerged from the ferry holding on to the arm of a man. Daniel estimated that Solveig's mustachioed companion was almost as tall as he was, and was considerably younger than Solveig. The trio wore matching blue sweatshirts that said Norway in English. Overstock from one of her shops, Daniel assumed.

Solveig spotted Daniel. "How good of you to meet us. It is so nice to see you again."

Unsure how to respond, he grunted, and braced himself for a hug that did not materialize. "You did not mention that Sarah was coming with you."

Solveig took a deep breath. "Did you wait very long?"

"Oh no, I guessed that you would be on the last ferry. You must be tired after a long journey." He immediately wondered why he said such a thing. It could have been a short, relaxing trip.

"Yes, what a trip. We stayed last night at the hotel in Tvedestrand. Have you stayed there?"

Tvedestrand was less than an hour away he remembered. "No, I never stayed there," he said flatly.

Solveig took Daniel by the arm. "Come, I want to introduce you." She guided him toward her dark haired companion who was looking down on a knoll of assorted luggage. Sarah was standing by the seawall, frowning and watching the progress of a passing swan. "Daniel Nordal, this is Thomas Fielding."

"Call me Tom," the man said as he pressed Daniel's hand.

Daniel ventured a greeting in Norwegian.

"What?" Tom squinted and turned to Solveig.

"You will need to speak English for Tom," Solveig said in Norwegian. "And of course, you know Sarah."

"Of course. We should both speak English." He turned to where Sarah stood. "Hello Sarah." She did not answer, but stared out over the Sound.

"Sarah, someone is talking to you," Tom said.

Sarah twisted around so that her back was toward Daniel. So this is Sarah's father, Daniel thought. He searched for, and experimented with a few sentences for Tom. He settled on, "I hope you had a good trip." Tom shrugged, and Daniel turned to Solveig. "I brought my boat to take the luggage."

"What?" asked Tom. "Is this Lyngør or do we have to go somewhere else?"

"Lyngør is a community spread over four islands. The island you are going to is just a little walk over a footbridge," Daniel said. He surveyed the luggage and wondered why the ferry did not capsize. It would take more than one trip to haul their belongings, and he hoped that Tom did not want a ride.

"Are you hungry after your trip?" Daniel asked them. Solveig and Tom looked at each other as if Daniel had lapsed into an obscure dialect. He decided to isolate one of them, so he chose Tom. "There is a fine restaurant here. You can have a good meal while I bring your luggage to the cottage in the boat."

Tom turned to Solveig. "Am I missing something? A boat? I thought there was a bridge."

Solveig patted Tom's arm. "Everything is taken care of."

Sarah spun around and folded her arms. "I don't want to walk."

"Stop it," said Tom. He turned to Solveig and grinned. "A luggage boat. How very exotic."

Solveig rolled her eyes.

Daniel nodded toward The Blue Lantern. "The fish is very good."

"Blah," said Sarah.

"There is a museum inside as well," Daniel said, and looked expectantly at Tom. "There are relics from a naval battle that was fought in these waters. A British man-of-war engaged a Norwegian frigate." Encouraged by signs of interest from Tom, Daniel continued. "Norway was once under Danish rule you know, and Denmark supported Napoleon."

"Yes, yes. I see how that could happen." Tom stroked his chin. "Who won the engagement?"

Before Daniel could answer, Solveig pulled him aside and whispered in Norwegian. "I hope you will forgive Sarah. She acts different when Tom is around."

"Of course the man-of-war would have the advantage," Tom said.

Solveig tugged a little harder on Daniel's arm. "I suppose you are wondering about Tom?"

"You guessed it. The man-of-war won," Daniel said in what he realized was an unnaturally loud voice.

"Does having Tom here make you uncomfortable?" Solveig asked in Norwegian.

"Of course not. It was part of a war that happened many years ago. Nobody is taking sides here."

"Never mind," Solveig said and sighed. She continued in Norwegian. "Tom is a good man, and Sarah does not have a mother." She paused. "And I am alone."

"Coming Solveig?" Tom was already at the restaurant door.

"The luggage will be too much for you. Tom can help," Solveig said. "How thoughtless of me. Have you had dinner?"

"I am not hungry, and do not bother Tom about the luggage. I work best at my own pace."

"How can I thank you? Please join us here later for coffee."

Daniel estimated that it would take four trips to transport their luggage. That is just as well, he decided. He would rather not join them at the restaurant. The work went slowly, and he imagined that Thomas Fielding was sales representative for a lead shot company.

On the last trip, Daniel wrestled one particularly heavy suitcase from the boat to the seawall. His arms shook from the strain; the boat heeled and the suitcase plunged into the Sound. Perhaps he would be able to borrow a grapple at the marina in the morning. Maybe, he would be lucky, and maybe Tom would forgive him.

It took another thirty minutes to shuttle the luggage from the seawall to the upstairs apartment. He felt worn out, and needed to use his inhaler. After resting for ten minutes, he felt obliged to go to The Blue Lantern. Yes, he decided, he was obliged to report the accident as soon as possible.

When Daniel entered the restaurant, he saw that Solveig had her arms folded, and she was facing away from Tom with a scowl on her face. Tom had pushed his plate to the centre of the table, and was drumming the table with his fingers. Sarah sat with her neck folded over the back of her chair, looking at the ceiling. Daniel knew at once that his timing was bad, so he tried to back out through the door unseen. But Solveig spotted him, and waved for him to join them. Her face softened and she called for an extra coffee. "We are not having dessert, but if you would like some . . ."

Tom drummed his fingers a little faster, and looked intently at Solveig. "How was I to know the proprietor understood English?"

"Where do you think you are?" Solveig asked. "In some third world country?" She turned to Daniel and said in a low voice in Norwegian. "Tom said some things about the museum. It was very embarrassing."

"What?" Tom asked.

"I think they have a fine museum here," Solveig said in a loud voice.

Sarah snapped her head back into a vertical position. "I want to go home."

This would not be a good time to introduce the subject of submerged luggage to Tom, Daniel decided. He sipped his coffee and wished he were back in the skerries of Lillesand. Tom left the table to take another look at the museum display, and Daniel saw his chance to check Solveig's reaction. "The large blue suitcase with an airline tag? Was that Tom's?" He asked in a whisper.

"Yes, I asked Tom to pack light. Did you have trouble with it? Oh my, you should not be working like that."

Daniel hesitated. "It fell into the Sound. Naturally I will try to retrieve it in the morning."

Solveig's eyes widened. She brought her hands to her mouth and sputtered. At first Daniel thought she was crying, but then she howled, and her laughter echoed through the restaurant. Like a spreading fire, laughter caught hold. Daniel sipped coffee to suppress his urge, but he lost control and sprayed coffee across the table. Sarah started to giggle, and clapped her hands. Everyone in the restaurant looked their way and vicariously shared their merriment.

Tom came back to the table with a grin on his face. "What did I miss?" The question provoked a new round of laughter and giggles.

Solveig took a deep breath. "Well, Daniel sprayed coffee on the table."

Tom raised an eyebrow. "Nordic humour, I don't understand it." Sarah started to giggle again, while Tom frowned and shook his head.

Daniel cleared his throat. "Mr. Fielding, I have something to tell you about your—"

"Could I ask you a big favour?" Solveig asked while placing her hand on Daniel's arm. "Would you mind going ahead and turning the outside lights on?" The hand on his arm became a claw that squeezed with each word she spoke.

After a hurried breakfast, Daniel grabbed a glass tumbler and went to the seawall. He crawled into his skiff, and pressed the bottom of the tumbler into the water. As he looked through the crude looking glass, he spotted the suitcase on a ledge three feet from the surface. The water in the Sound was cold, but Daniel judged he could tolerate it for a minute or two. He stripped his shirt off, took a deep breath, and draped his upper body over the edge of the gunwale. When he stretched his arms out under the water, he discovered that the suitcase was just a few inches beyond his reach. Just a few more inches, he willed. He stretched again, and just as his fingertips touched the luggage, he felt his legs slip over the gunwale, and he pushed the suitcase deeper. With his lungs aching and his whole body submerged, he pulled himself along the rough surface of the seawall to the surface. Daniel crawled from the water and sat shivering on the wall. There was a noise behind him; he turned and saw Sarah.

"Could you see it?" Sarah asked. He nodded, and was about to explain what happened, when Sarah ran back into the cottage.

Since he was already wet, he decided to make another attempt. He removed his shoes, took a deep breath, and jumped into the water. First, he rolled forward, and then he pulled himself hand over hand down the rock face. The suitcase was easy to find, but it was too heavy to lift while swimming. Driven by air hunger, he climbed the seawall carrying the suitcase. At last, choking and coughing, he broke the surface.

For a minute he remained suspended. One hand clutched the top of the wall, holding his weight, and the other barely held the suitcase. Then he heard a gasp. Looking up, he saw the threesome. Solveig's jaw was almost on her chest, Tom was shaking his head, and Sarah appeared to be transfixed.

"I cannot seem to pull myself out," Daniel said in a hoarse voice.

"Isn't anyone going to help him?" Sarah asked.

Tom seemed to wake from a dream. "Oh, of course." He removed his sweatshirt, and spread it on the ground. After kneeling carefully on the shirt, he reached with both hands for Daniel's wrist, and started to pull. He moaned with the effort. "Why don't you use your other hand on the wall?" Then the suitcase came into Tom's view just below the surface. "Oh, my God!" The bag—full of water—became too heavy to support as it rose from the water. Tom and Daniel struggled for a few seconds, but the weight of the water forced open the latch. Shirts, slacks, socks, and underwear, spilled out and drifted on the waters of Lyngør Sound. Tom gasped and almost dropped Daniel. It was obvious to Daniel, from Tom's reaction and the fear on Solveig's face, that they had not discussed the suitcase.

Barely able to speak, Daniel crawled, wheezing and shivering, over the rim of the seawall to collapse on the grass. He attempted an apology for the luggage, but Solveig stopped him, and helped him to his feet. "A hot shower at once," she said firmly, and led him to the cottage. As he entered the cottage, he could hear Tom complaining, and Sarah giggling.

Daniel made heavy use of his inhaler, showered, and wrapped himself in a down comforter. The shivering continued, until he had finished two tins of chicken soup that Solveig heated for him. She reported that Sarah had amused herself by fishing Tom's clothes from the Sound with a stick. "The clothes can be washed. And neither Tom nor the clothes will be worse for the experience."

As soon as Solveig left, Daniel fell into a deep sleep that carried him into the afternoon—until the phone rang. "You do not sound very well," Ingrid said.

"I just woke from a nap."

"You have always said how little sleep you need. What is wrong?"

"I am fine, and the work is going well. I should be back in Lillesand before long." Daniel sighed. "That is where my mind is."

"Well, I am not convinced that you are well. Listen, I do not have any work this Saturday. So, with a couple of days off, I thought I would sail to Lyngør. It will be a change of scenery for me, and I can sleep on the boat."

"That will be wonderful. Sarah will be glad to see you."

"Sarah?"

"Yes, Sarah is here and her father too. And of course Solveig."

Daniel waited for a response, but none came. "Are you still there?"

"Oh, yes. Well, that should be interesting. I will stop at Knudsen's and get you some raisin rolls."

Daniel asked her about Birk and the island, but she had nothing to report. After he set down the phone, he began to have mixed feelings about the visit. It was getting a little too crowded on Lyngør for Daniel's comfort.

14

Daniel dreamed of the island where his wife and daughter perished. He arrived there on a boat that had no helm, no sail, and no motor. Unseen hands urged him from the boat to the dock, and when he turned back, the boat was gone. On the bluff, he found nothing but ash where the cabin once stood. Falling to his knees, Daniel opened his mouth to scream, but all he could hear was the moaning wind. An invisible force lifted him, transported him over the island, and suspended him over the cove. The hill that once sloped gently to the bay, now imprisoned by a retaining wall of stone, gave way to a half-dozen cabins. Children laughing and shouting had gathered around a blazing fire. The older children were grabbing wood from a nearby pile. One tall boy held a board with words painted red. Daniel realized at once that this was part of the bench he made. The memorial to Linda and Emma. With a shout, the boy lifted the board over his head to throw it into the fire. Daniel clawed at the air trying to stop the youth. "No, no," Daniel said with a groan, and he woke drenched in sweat. There could be no doubt—the dream was a sign. Ingrid will be here today, he remembered; he will return with her. Just to check. Just to make sure.

It calmed Daniel to have a plan, so he turned his thoughts to Tom's suitcase. He had not talked with Tom since his clothes floated in the Sound; it was time to make amends. Breakfast—he would make breakfast for everyone. Solveig and her guests were still sleeping. What could he do in advance? A craving for coffee fished an idea from his mind. An idea so fantastic, he congratulated himself on his cleverness. He would boil coffee ten times stronger that usual, then, when served, he would only need to add hot water. In short order, he counted out two hundred coffee beans, ground them extra fine, and had them boiling in a pint of water.

After fifteen minutes of boiling, he heard someone stirring upstairs. His timing was perfect. The stir became a rumble, and he heard muffled voices and then a door burst open. He could see activity in the garden, and was surprised to see Solveig half-carrying Sarah away from the building. Tom came into view, stumbling, and rubbing his eyes. Daniel was pleased to see everyone up and active, so he went into the garden to greet them. "Good Morning." Daniel said in as cheery a voice as he could muster. "I do not like to sleep late either. Well now, I have some fresh coffee waiting. Come in, come in." Solveig and Tom looked at each other with blank expressions, and Sarah went to her father and buried her face under his arm. The trio hesitated, then walked slowly, following Daniel into the cottage. Solveig remained by the door, and swung it to and fro to create a draught in the apartment.

"There's no fire," Sarah said.

Tom glared at her. "Sarah!"

Solveig shook Tom's arm. "We should have told you Daniel. Tom and I are cutting back on coffee. Yes Tom?" She turned to Tom and raised her eyebrows. "Yes Tom? He grunted and pushed her hand away.

"I understand," Daniel said. "I would be pleased if you would join me for breakfast."

Tom and Solveig glanced at each other. "We need to freshen up a bit," Solveig said. "Yes, we got up rather quickly." Tom guided Sarah away from the stove where she was poking at the coffee sludge with a fork.

"Come back whenever you are ready," Daniel said. When he was alone, Daniel set to work, laying out a traditional Norwegian breakfast. He set out a large brick of brown goat cheese, several types of pickled herring, lingonberry preserves, and flat bread. The food display seemed poor, so he added Jarlsberg cheese, canned mackerel, and oat crackers. Not good enough he decided, so he added cloudberry preserves and sardines. Troubled by the miserly appearance of the table, he emptied out his refrigerator and cupboard whether or not the items were suitable for breakfast.

Tom returned first. He yawned, looked at the food and asked, "Would you have some corn flakes?"

Daniel shook his head. Now I have done it, Daniel thought, but at least he is talking to me. "It is not far to the grocer and my boat is right here at—"

"You will do no such thing," Solveig said from the doorway. She entered and surveyed the food. "Oh, a real Norwegian breakfast." Daniel smiled and invited her to help herself. "Look at all those calories. I cannot eat like that anymore."

"What do you eat now?" Daniel asked.

"If I eat anything in the morning now, it is fat-free yogurt."

He had created a disaster; he wondered why he ever bothered. There was still Sarah. If she will eat something, it would not be a total loss. "What does Sarah like?"

"All she will eat for breakfast are toaster pastries," Tom said. "Only the frosted ones with strawberry filling."

Daniel sighed. "There is only one thing to do. There is a store on Outer Lyngør."

"No, no." Solveig held up her hands. "A dab of cloudberry preserves on a cracker would be nice, and I am sure Tom would like to try some goat cheese. As for Sarah, how could she resist lingonberry preserves?" She turned to Tom and pointed to the brown goat cheese. "Try this, it is called gjetøst."

Tom pretended to gag, and he walked from the room. "Please forgive him," Solveig said. She threw up her hands and followed Tom.

Daniel added a spoon of coffee sludge to a cup of hot

water, but he did not drink it. He lost interest in eating too, and decided to put everything away. As he rose, he saw Sarah standing in the doorway. "Would you like something to eat?"

"Solveig said you had some berry jam."

"I certainly do Sarah." He waved his hand over the table. "Several kinds." He moved the preserves, flatbread, and crackers to one end of the table. "Please help yourself." Sarah selected oat crackers with lingonberry preserves. She followed her first cracker with three more; each one carried the maximum capacity of lingonberries. As she ate, Daniel's appetite returned, and he piled lingonberry preserves as high as he dared on an oat cracker. He promised Sarah that he would try to find toaster pastries for her, but she told a grinning Daniel that lingonberry preserves were better. A great sigh of relief came, as he had no toaster, and he could set aside plans for heating slabs of frozen pastry in a frying pan.

"How long are you going to be in Norway?" Daniel asked. She shrugged, "What about school?"

"I have junk with me I'm supposed to look at." Without another word, and with a cracker in her hand, Sarah left the apartment. Soon after she left, she knocked on his window and pointed excitedly toward the waterfront. He looked where she pointed and saw Ingrid's sloop coming about in the Sound. As fast as he could, he piled the cheeses into the refrigerator, and ran to the seawall where he stood next to Sarah and waved.

In a few minutes, the sloop was at anchor three hundred yards from shore, and Ingrid was climbing from her dinghy. She greeted Sarah, and thrust a bag at Daniel. "This should keep you alive." He opened the bag and counted a dozen raisin rolls. "They are from yesterday, but since you dip them in acid, it should not matter. You can use them a week from now." She turned to look at her boat. "I do not think I should stay at anchor there, but I am not sure of the water depth by the seawall. What are you laughing at?"

"I am very familiar with the water depth at the seawall," Daniel said. Sarah started to giggle. "I will explain later," he added.

Ingrid cocked her head and squinted. "I better look for a proper dock."

"There is a community dock a short distance from here where I have seen boats with a greater draught than yours. I will walk along the shore to guide you."

With Ingrid's sloop following in the Sound, Daniel strolled along the seawall with a bag of raisin rolls under his arm. Just when he was about to converge with the sloop at the dock, Daniel noticed Sarah, frowning and shuffling thirty feet behind him. He turned and waved. "Hurry Sarah, we need your help."

"What for?"

"Ingrid needs someone to catch a rope. I am not very good at it."

Sarah shrugged and quickened her pace. At the dock, Ingrid was close enough so that she could have handed the line to Sarah, but she went through the motions as if she were throwing it a great distance. Sarah caught the line, and Daniel showed her how to tie it to a cleat on the dock. "Ingrid has one more line to throw, and you can handle it by yourself." When Sarah secured the second line, Ingrid came ashore and gave her a hug. While Daniel picked covertly at a raisin roll, Sarah darted off to announce Ingrid's arrival. It occurred to Daniel that he had failed to tell Solveig that Ingrid was coming.

If Solveig was surprised to see Ingrid, she did not show it. Solveig introduced Tom to Ingrid, and suggested that they all meet later at The Blue Lantern for lunch. Sarah pleaded to go sailing, so Ingrid promised she would take her in the afternoon.

At Ingrid's request, Daniel took her to see the work he was doing. "You are amazing Daniel. If word got out, there would be a high demand for your skills. Do you like doing this?"

"I used to like it. I even enjoyed it."

"And now?"

"Sometimes, when I get very involved in what I am doing, I forget about things. Then it is almost like old times again." He thought about the dream he had, and was about to relate it, when Ingrid took his arm.

"Now I am glad you came here. At first, I was worried." She looked up at his face. "It seems that we have the rest of the morning to ourselves. Would you care to show me around the island?"

A cool breeze blew from the Sound as they walked toward Holmen. Daniel talked about the suitcase in the Sound, and his attempt to make breakfast. Ingrid shook her head in wonder. "You sounded terrible on the phone, but now that I see you . . ." She laughed. "Maybe an occasional dip in the Sound is good for you. As for breakfast, it seems you can get off easy as a host. Just get some corn flakes and yogurt. They can bring their own coffee."

"No, no. They do not drink coffee any more."

Ingrid groaned. "You are so thick headed Daniel Nordal."

Daniel pictured the dishevelled look of the group in the garden, and Sarah reporting that there was no fire. "Well yes, now that I think about it. Coffee—concentrated coffee!" He laughed so hard that he had to stop walking and tears ran down his face.

Ingrid squeezed his arm. "It is good to hear you laugh. You used to laugh often." They walked over the bridge to Holmen, and Ingrid began to play with the end of her braid. "Do you think this job will take very long?"

"Maybe a few months, maybe a little longer."

"When Solveig leaves you will be isolated again, and that worries me." They walked past the post office and the community bulletin board. "What does Tom do for a living?"

"I have no idea."

"Can you see? Even when you have people around you—you isolate yourself."

"I am, what I am," Daniel said in a barely audible voice. "We make a right turn here." Daniel cleared his throat. "Have you heard any news about Birk and the island?"

Ingrid twisted the end of her braid and sighed. "I guess it is progress when Birk is not the first thing you talk about." She looked at the sky and took a deep breath. "I saw the student in town a few weeks ago. Yes, Sondre was his name, and he was getting ready to go back to school. According to what he said, it has been very quiet on the island this summer. That is all I can tell you. What is that building?"

"An elementary school. Older children leave the island on school days."

"Promise me something? No more talk about Birk or the island this weekend?"

After a long silence Daniel said, "I would like to go back with you to Lillesand. Just to check on things."

"No, take a bus." She walked faster.

Confusion, pain, and anger swelled together, and just as quickly, crashed into despair. Should he ask her why she turned on him? No, in his heart he knew the answer, and he was not ready to hear it from her.

"You want to live on that island forever. Alone. Yes?" She raised her chin and spoke without looking at Daniel. "Are you afraid to leave? What will happen? The island was never yours. So what are you trying to do?"

What reply could he make? He could not give a simple answer to Ingrid, because he had no simple answer for himself. He slowed his pace, and Ingrid pushed ahead.

Ingrid stopped abruptly so that Daniel nearly collided with her. "What in God's name am I doing?" She shook her head as if there were a viper in her hair. "I thought things could change," she murmured. She turned to face Daniel. "Please forgive me. It is your business alone, what you do and think." She took a deep breath. "If you want to come with me to Lillesand, you are welcome to do so. Oh Daniel, the reason I get so frustrated with you is that I care what happens to you." Her gaze softened, and she spoke softly. "I care about you."

The wound healed, and the scar vanished, yet a vague fear began to creep over him. It was obvious, even to Daniel, that Ingrid expected some kind of response. But what he felt, he could not identify, so he remained silent. And the silence stretched on, and became uncomfortable, until he knew he must say something—anything. "Would you like to see more of Lyngør?" With a look of resignation, Ingrid turned to continue on the path. *I care about you* played over and over in his mind.

Beyond the schoolhouse, they turned to descend a steep path to the shore. "You like to walk when you think. Do you not?" Ingrid asked. "And you dread lunch today. Oh yes, there will be too many people. You are only comfortable with Solveig and me because we knew you as children. And, you would like for me to be quiet now, so you can think. Oh, but I see I am making you uncomfortable again. So Daniel, do I know you?"

"You know me all too well." Daniel forced a laugh. "But you are always welcome company Ingrid. I promise. I will not speak anymore today of Birk or the island." They walked on every trail and path on the islands of Odden and Holmen, some more than once. They walked for the remainder of the morning, but Daniel could not hold on to a thought except to replay Ingrid's words—*I care about you.*

Satisfied that Tom dominated the conversation, Daniel remained quiet and picked at his lunch. He listened while Ingrid asked Tom about his occupation, and he listened to the reply. A seemingly endless description of what a drug company representative does. Talk turned to the mind-numbing details of drug trials, followed by a vigorous description of how anti-reflux medications work. "There is gold in reflux," Tom declared. All of which, Daniel decided, was license to allow his mind to drift.

Everyone except Sarah pretended interest in the shutting down of stomach acid pumps. She entertained herself by subdividing a boiled potato into ever-smaller fragments. Daniel found her activity to be far more interesting than

Tom's monologue. Daniel sliced, and cross-sliced his potato in quick strokes. Sarah saw his response, and accepted the challenge. She had her potato looking like meal in two minutes. No match for the ten-year-old, Daniel surrendered with a covert nod. She mouthed the word "bor-ing," left the table, and paced on the outdoor deck.

"I know what to do," Ingrid said. Daniel watched Ingrid join Sarah on the deck, where, placing a hand on the girls shoulder, led her to the ice cream freezer. Sarah fished around with her arm, and pulled out an ice cream sandwich. Adding to Daniel's distress, they both remained on the deck, happily free from the terrors of acid reflux. As if she read his mind, Ingrid looked his way and winked.

Daniel was lightning-struck when Solveig said, "I think I will see what the girls are up to."

While Tom droned on about the problems of introducing a drug into a country with a national health system, Daniel tried to catch Ingrid's attention with eye movements. Tom then inquired if Daniel had an eye disorder. For a moment, Tom was distracted by the proprietor. It was long enough for Daniel to give Ingrid his best please-rescue-me look. Ingrid grinned, said something to Solveig, and both women looked at Daniel and laughed. After an agonizing minute, Ingrid came to the table and announced that it was time to set sail.

Tom paid the bill, and the group paraded across the bridge to Odden. Though Tom continued his monologue, Daniel discovered that acid reflux disease seemed less oppressive in the open air.

As they approached the cottage, Tom and Solveig exchanged whispers and winks. "You know," Solveig said, "I think it would be better if Sarah goes sailing without Tom and me." She patted her stomach "Too much motion after a big meal. I have a sensitive stomach you know." She looked expectantly at Tom.

"Oh yes," Tom said while rubbing his stomach. "I have a sensitive stomach too."

"Acid reflux disease," Daniel said in a low voice to Ingrid. "Talking about it will bring it on." He felt Ingrid's elbow in his side.

"Sarah, do you mind if we don't go?" asked Tom.

"Who cares." Sarah walked off toward the dock.

"Sarah!"

After Solveig and Tom retired to the cottage, Ingrid said, "Maybe it is well that it will be just us."

15

Sarah was eager to demonstrate what she remembered, so without asking, she took charge of the jib sheets while the two adults remained in the stern. They sailed up and down the Sound, and for Sarah's sake, practised turning through the wind. The young girl proved to be quick and adept at the manoeuvre. In less than an hour, she went beyond the mechanics of sail handling to fine-tuning the jib for maximum performance.

"She is a natural," Ingrid said.

Daniel nodded. "Just like you were at her age."

"Oh, did you notice me then?"

"Sarah," Daniel called, "let us see how you do turning downwind."

Ingrid gave the order for Sarah, and spun the wheel. Then in a low voice said, "You were not listening to Tom during lunch. What were you thinking about?"

"Of course I listened to every word." He laughed. "No, I was thinking that maybe it is not a good idea if I return to Lillesand with you now."

"This morning I was too hard on you."

"No, I want to make faster progress on Solveig's shop."

"So you can give your full attention to the island."

"How long are we going to go in a straight line?" Sarah asked.

Ingrid changed the sloop's heading. "Stand by to jibe." Sarah freed a jib sheet from its cleat, and looked expectantly at Ingrid. "Jibe-oh," said Ingrid as she turned the wheel hard. "Wonderful, you can crew for me anytime."

"Maybe I can finish everything in a month," Daniel said.

"I thought Solveig expected that you would stay here until next spring."

"Maybe she wanted someone to keep an eye on things, but there is no need for that on Lyngør." He made an insignificant adjustment to the mainsail. "I need to think. I cannot seem to think clearly in Lillesand. Maybe another month here will help." He adjusted the sail again. "Maybe I have been wrong."

Ingrid's eyes left the sails to find his. "What are you saying?"

"About the past. About the future. What to do. I do not know. Sometimes I feel lost."

"Where is your home?" Ingrid asked gently.

Daniel remained quiet for a while. He wiped spray from his eyes. "I do not know."

"Hey you guys, what's next?" Sarah asked.

"Switch places with me," Daniel said. "Let us see you work the mainsail."

Positioning himself so that he faced away from the breeze, Daniel felt warm and comfortable. Everything seemed right. Why should that be? If only he could feel as he did that moment—forever. Ingrid and Sarah were chatting and laughing, and in Daniel's mind, they became Linda and Emma: they were sailing on Long Island Sound. He tried to hold the image, but it slipped away. The present is not so bad, he decided, just as it is now. Just as it is now.

On return to Odden, Ingrid promised another sailing lesson in the morning; Sarah ran into the cottage to tell Solveig. After they secured the sloop, Ingrid said, "We have the rest of the afternoon to ourselves. Have I seen all of Lyngør?"

"We can take my skiff across the Sound to Outer Lyngør. I have never gone beyond the shore path. Perhaps we can explore the island together."

They walked along the shore of Outer Lyngør and admired the well-kept cottages, and then they turned to follow a path that bisected the island and emerged on a rugged coast near a lighthouse. At Ingrid's suggestion, they sat on a rock by the shore.

"Sarah seemed to enjoy herself this afternoon," Ingrid said. "You looked like you were going to fall asleep when Sarah came to the stern. Tired?"

"I do not know if you are ready to hear this," Daniel said with a chuckle. "I was actually content."

Ingrid pulled her braid forward and twisted its end. "And now?"

Gently, Daniel removed her hand from her braid. "Why do you worry on my account? But yes, I feel content now. I have to confess that I dreaded the coming of this weekend. Your visit would slow my work and . . ."

"Distract you?"

"A good way to put it."

"Did your fears come true?"

"On close examination, there was nothing to fear." Daniel picked up a rock and threw it into the sea. "I cannot put it in plain words, but I feel better right now, than I have felt in a long time." He picked up another rock and discarded it. "I feel at peace." Daniel shrugged. "I am sorry Ingrid; I cannot explain myself very well."

Ingrid twisted around on the rock to face Daniel. "You have explained yourself very well."

After a long silence, Daniel asked, "Do you have plans for dinner?"

"I did not know there was more than one place to eat on Lyngør." Ingrid grinned. "No, I have no plans."

"We do not have to go to The Blue Lantern. We have a boat; we could go to Gjeving or Risør. There would be many choices in Risør. And, I have herring and flatbread at the cottage."

"No herring for dinner thank you, and I have had enough boating for today. Going to The Blue Lantern would mean meeting with the others, and talk of stomach acid again."

There would have to be a graceful way out, Daniel decided. It was obvious that Ingrid did not want to dine with him. The contentment of the afternoon seemed to drain away. "It has been a busy day, and being on the water makes me sleepy." Feigning a yawn, he waited for Ingrid to agree.

"I thought you asked me to dinner. Did you change your mind?"

Was that a wink? He could not be sure. Asking her if she had plans for dinner was not the same as asking her to dinner. Or was it? What did she assume? What did she want? Maybe she wanted to make it easy for him to ask. Certainly, he had made a fool of himself by yawning. What could he do about that? *She is smiling—she must not be taking it seriously. She is waiting.* "No," he said cautiously. "I did not change my mind." Her smile seemed tender as he spoke, and he felt her squeeze his arm. A tidal wave of contentment engulfed him.

"I have a suggestion," Ingrid said. "In the sloop I have a generous wedge of Jarlsberg cheese, a reasonably fresh loaf of bread, and several bottles of beer. The menu is simple, but the view is good, and there will be no talk of acid reflux."

Daniel felt Ingrid lean against him, and when he tried to answer, he felt his throat thicken. So, he returned her smile, and gave her a weak nod.

"Sometimes simple is best, yes?" Receiving no answer, she continued. "Have you ever thought about what our lives would be like if we had never left Lillesand?"

"Our lives? You stayed. Perhaps that would have been better for me as well."

Ingrid laughed. "Do you think all I did was sit by the sea-wall in Lillesand since childhood?"

How thoughtless he must appear. Never asking. As if her life did not matter. Yes, thoughtless and selfish. Of course he could not ask now; it would be too obvious. Was it his imagination, or was the pressure on his arm increasing?

"That yawn of yours?" Ingrid shook her head. "Not very good."

They laughed together, and the laughter, it seemed to Daniel, absolved him of wrong.

Ingrid repositioned herself on the rock, and asked softly, "Shall we go?" Because Ingrid's feet did not reach the ground, Daniel stood and extended his hand to assist her, and as they walked away, their hands remained joined.

They spent the evening on the deck of Ingrid's sloop where Daniel resolved to give no thought to himself. The mystery of Ingrid's life became important to him, and he encouraged her to share it.

She spoke of her apprenticeship with a master boat builder from Risør, and of their mutual frustration with each other.

Ingrid became engaged to a fellow apprentice, a young man from Grimstad who, it turned out, kept a mistress on the side. Breaking the engagement, she left for Oslo to seek employment, and to distance herself from Lillesand. Attracted to the club scene, she fell in with a group of university students whose principle focus was partying and sex. In Oslo, she never acquired a job or an apartment of her own. When the summer came, a student invited her to travel with him to Scotland. They spent the nights in the pubs of Edinburgh, and the days shivering in Holyrood Park. One rainy day, stoned, seeking shelter and dodging the police in Waverley Station, Ingrid decided she had enough, and returned alone to Lillesand. Though expecting a warm and forgiving reception, she found an angry and cold father who would not let her return home. By begging and pleading, she resumed an uneasy relationship with the boat builder. "I gave all of my energy to learn my craft. At night, when I could no longer hold a tool, I fell asleep in whatever boat I was working on, but my tutor was never satisfied. Sometimes at night, my ex-fiancé would come around . . ."

"Oh Ingrid, I am so sorry."

"*No*, do not feel sorry for me." Shaking, she stood and wrapped her arms across her chest. "The wind is turning cold. I must go below."

Unsure of what to say, Daniel nodded and watched her move toward the cabin hatch.

Who was this girl from his childhood? Was she friend or stranger—this woman so full of hurt, yet so strong? She was there for him, but who had been there for her? Why had he never seen—never asked? *I care about you,* she had said. He felt he was just touching the edge of understanding. Tears obscured his vision. A sense of loss descended on Daniel as she disappeared into the cabin. "I should not leave you alone like this."

"Then come below," Daniel heard from the dark hatchway.

At first, Daniel perceived total darkness, but after a short time, he discerned Ingrid standing by a port looking out at the Sound. From behind her, he placed his hand on her shoulder. His hand trailed across her back as she turned to face him so that now his arm embraced her; it seemed only natural to bring his other arm to her waist. Leaning toward her, he tasted salt, and felt the flutter of an eyelid on his lips. Her arms encircled his waist; hands moved up his back and pressed her body against his, and he felt the gentle tide of her breathing. Repeating her name softly like a mantra, he drew her tighter in his arms—he would never be close enough. This was where he belonged; nothing else would ever matter. He knew at that moment; he found peace. Ingrid moved her hands to his face, lifted her head, and they merged—first with a kiss, and later, on a narrow bunk in the moonlight, with their whole being.

The world moved in slow motion. Sight, sound, and the

passage of time became a blur. Daniel sat by the seawall at the cottage, captivated by the play of morning light on water. In time, his aching limbs brought him to the present. Stretching, he looked across at Outer Lyngør as for the first time. The old community was so beautiful; the neat white building, and the bold red of the Norwegian flags. Ingrid should be awake by now, he decided. What a beautiful morning, to follow such a glorious night. Yes, Ingrid would want to share this too.

The community dock, hidden from the cottage by a curve of the shoreline, was less than a minute away for the long-striding carpenter. Ingrid's sloop was gone. Gone from the dock, and nowhere in sight. Perhaps, he reasoned, she went to Gjeving or Risør for supplies. But no, it is Sunday; stores are closed. If she did not sail past the cottage, then she must have headed to sea. Of course, she is enjoying the morning, and celebrating the night in her own way. And she promised Sarah another sailing lesson. She will return.

Daniel set out cheese and crackers for breakfast, but he just looked at the food without interest. Someone knocked on the door. Ingrid? He jumped up and dashed to the door.

"May I borrow some of your lingonberry preserves, and some oat crackers?" Solveig asked. "It is all Sarah will eat for breakfast now. Please come and join us upstairs. There is plenty to eat and Sarah asked for you." Reluctantly, Daniel followed Solveig; he sat with the trio but did not eat.

The phone rang, and Solveig took the call in the kitchen. After a short time, Solveig called out, "Sarah, come here, Ingrid wants to talk with you." While Sarah took the phone, Solveig came to Daniel. She had a deep furrow in her forehead. "She called to apologize to Sarah about the sailing lesson. Did you know she left Lyngør?"

"I need to talk with her too." He left the table and went to where the sad-faced girl was talking.

"Yeah, it's okay," Sarah said into the phone. "Somebody else wants to talk." She threw the handset on the counter where Daniel scooped it up.

"Hello Ingrid," Daniel said with a shaking voice.

"I have to go now. Forgive me Daniel." The line went dead. He slumped into the nearest chair and buried his face in his hands. There was the sound of a door closing—he looked up and found himself alone with Solveig.

"Did she go back to Lillesand?"

He shrugged. "She has a mobile phone on the boat."

Solveig sat close to him. "We called at your apartment last night."

Sarah's sobs came through the wall. "There are small sailboats for hire at Gjeving," Daniel said. "I will not disappoint her."

"Do you want to talk about it?"

"I can leave for Gjeving now."

Solveig shook his arm. "I am not talking about Sarah. She will survive."

"I should check with Tom before I say anything to Sarah."

In a steady breeze, Daniel and Sarah set out in a sloop-rigged, twelve-foot sailboat. With its weighted keel, Daniel was comfortable that it would be forgiving if handled poorly. When Sarah tired of tacking, she practised jibing. When that bored her, Daniel threw a life jacket into the Sound and told her it was a drowning man. At first, she ran into, or missed the imagined victim by a wide margin, but she had quick reflexes and a good sense of wind direction. After twenty minutes of practice, a drowning person would have a good chance of recovery with Sarah in command.

After two hours, Daniel asked her if she wanted to rest, but she declined. So, he put her in charge, and she sailed where she pleased. She was curious about Outer Lyngør, so they docked there and explored. When exploration bored her, Daniel allowed her to manage the boat without assistance. She would do well by herself in good weather, he judged, but she would need help coming to a dock. They finished the sailing lesson at The Blue Lantern where Sarah had ice cream, and Daniel coffee. After bringing Sarah to the cottage, he returned the boat to Gjeving and retrieved his skiff.

He felt a strong urge to row, so he used his inhaler, and pulled for Outer Lyngør. Talking with Solveig was out of the question, so he spent the rest of the day on that island.

Avoiding the place where he sat with Ingrid the day before, he walked every path and trail over and over. The only way he could survive the coming night would be to collapse from exhaustion. He rowed to Odden in the moonlight, slipped into his apartment, and fell into a deep sleep.

Work would sustain him. He would take no breaks and give no thought to time. Solveig's project would be finished as soon as possible, and he would return to Lillesand. Certain that he could cut and install the shelving in one day he plunged ahead with all the energy he could find. Old rolls, with petrified raisins, dunked in cold coffee sustained him.

At midday, Solveig came to the shop to invite Daniel to join the group for lunch. He declined, claiming to have already eaten.

Late afternoon of the following day, while Daniel was framing one of the display counters, Tom knocked on the door and asked to talk. "I've been wondering," Tom said. "Well, actually Solveig has been wondering. Is everything all right here?"

"Very well Tom. I would not be surprised if the work is completed in one or two weeks at most."

"Well I . . . uh . . . Solveig isn't worried about the work. She said there's no hurry. Of course we hear you working."

"Naturally, the work requires some noise. Is it too much?"

"Oh no, it's not about the noise. We hear you working from

sunrise to long after sunset." Tom shrugged. "You don't come outside anymore. You don't seem to take breaks. Solveig said you were in the hospital not too long ago. Maybe you are working too hard."

"If I do not disturb you or Solveig, or of course Sarah, then I will continue as I have. In the long run, it will be less expensive for Solveig, and I can get on with some interests of my own."

"As you wish." Tom started to turn away. "Solveig would like it if you joined us at The Blue Lantern tonight."

Daniel declined and plunged back into his work. To allow his thoughts to drift from work would be unbearable. He would work until he dropped.

Long after sundown, Solveig came to the apartment holding a paper bag. "I heard you working. I hope you do not mind if I come in."

"Not at all." He gestured to the work he had completed. "You can see, the shop is coming together rather quickly."

"I see that Daniel. It all looks wonderful, but I did not come to check on your work." She held the bag out to him. "I wanted to bring you a slice of apple cake from the restaurant. You seemed fond of it."

"How very kind of you." He took the bag and placed it on a sawhorse. "To have with my coffee in the morning."

"Are you feeling well?"

This, he knew, was a follow up to Tom's inquiry. Perhaps she does not trust Tom to report his condition. He gave a curt nod.

"I called Ingrid today." She examined Daniel closely, and took a deep breath. "Like you, she speaks very little. I know this is none of my business, but...." She looked around the room, then at Daniel. "When you are ready, I am here to listen. You really must slow down. Promise me that?"

16

Two hours after sunrise, Daniel observed that Tom and Solveig were outside his window in the garden. Tom shook his head at something she said, and Solveig glared at him. He walked away and Solveig entered the shop.

"Please excuse the interruption. If I may, I have a big favour to ask. We are only going to be here four more days, and Sarah was hoping that she could go sailing again. Of course, I will pay for the boat and your time. It would mean so much to her, and it would give you a change of pace."

"Of course. Today if you wish, but it must be my treat."

Solveig clapped her hands together. "Wonderful! Sarah will be so happy."

They had lunch together at the Gjeving marina, and set out on the Sound for an afternoon of sailing. After a few practice manoeuvres, Daniel let Sarah handle the boat without his assistance, and to go where she chose within the confines of Lyngør Sound. At first, he found pleasure in watching her. She was relaxed yet always aware of her surroundings, the wind, and the trim of the sails. But then, his attention drifted.

There was no doubt; he drove Ingrid away. But how? He replayed every word, every act that they shared, but there were no answers. Everything had gone wrong. Of course, he should have stayed in Lillesand, but he could do nothing about that now. Why try anymore? It would be easy just to roll over the gunwale into the Sound—just another accident. But Sarah was there. He would have to focus on Sarah, and for now, he would survive. "It is time for a new lesson."

Daniel directed Sarah to practise bringing the boat along side of a dock. They worked together docking the boat repeatedly, from different directions and at different locations. Sarah missed her target a few times, and hit the dock hard a few times, but she did well for a beginner. When they tired of docking, he had her sail directly into the wind. The boat lost way, and he taught her how to regain control by backing the jib and letting the wind reposition the vessel.

From out in the Sound, they spotted Solveig and Tom standing by the cottage and waving. "Here is your chance to show them what you can do," Daniel said. Sail toward the cottage; then turn into the wind sharply, about twenty feet from the seawall." Accepting the challenge with enthusiasm, Sarah directed the boat toward the seawall at maximum speed. Daniel tensed, ready to grab the tiller, but Sarah completed the manoeuvre flawlessly.

Applause came from the shore, and Sarah pretended to be unaware. Then, to Daniel's surprise, Sarah invited Tom to come sail with her. He refused, and turned the invitation to Solveig who begged off. "Who cares," Sarah said and looked away from her father and Solveig, but Daniel could see that her eyes were wet. With hand signals and facial expression, Daniel attempted to convey Sarah's hurt to the pair.

After what appeared to be a heated exchange, Tom stood with folded arms and granite face while Solveig called, "You know, it would be a nice day for sailing. Mind if I come?"

When Sarah did not respond, Daniel said, "We would love to have you aboard. Meet us at the dock."

After helping Solveig board the small craft, Daniel settled himself in the bow. Sarah, Daniel decided, needed an affirmation of her skill. "Just pretend I am not here. Why not tack between here and Outer Lyngør. Then I am sure you can come alongside this dock without help." His words returned the smile to Sarah's face, and drained the colour from Solveig's. "You are in good hands with Sarah at the helm."

After thirty minutes in the Sound, Sarah approached the dock, but spilled the wind too soon. The stalled boat bobbed on the swell too far from the dock to secure a hold. "Perfect," Daniel said with a loud voice. "Just as we practised. The bow line is behind me. Do I have your permission to throw it to your father?"

Sarah cocked her head, and scrunched up one side of her face. After a few moments, she relaxed and said, "Yeah sure. Like we practised."

As Tom pulled the boat to the dock, Solveig declared, "Sarah, I would sail with you anywhere." And to Daniel she mouthed, *Thank you.* Daniel climbed ashore to secure the bow line to a cleat, and then he steadied the boat for Solveig. "Do you want to go out again Sarah?" Daniel asked. She stood and removed her life jacket. With one hand gripping the mast, she stretched out a leg onto the dock. Only the bow line held the boat, so the force of her leg striking the pier pivoted the boat away just as she released her hold on the mast. She tumbled forward; her head struck the dock, and she slipped into the water.

Frozen with horror, Daniel's mind replayed a different reality. Emma ran to the water. Emma struggled against the current. Linda raced across the cove and dove. He tried to run to them but his legs froze. They disappeared. "Emma, Emma, Oh God, Linda." Someone close shouted his name. Then a splash and a spray of water drew him back to the present. Solveig was in the Sound struggling to hold Sarah's head above water.

Another person thrashing in the water would not help he knew, so Daniel jumped to the boat and threw the main halyard to Solveig who held Sarah with one hand and took the halyard with the other. "Just hold on, do not pull." He took up the slack, and secured his end. Draping his body over the gunwale, he managed to grab Sarah under her arms. An inch at a time, he worked Sarah's upper body into the boat. Solveig reached for the boat. "No, the boat will tip. Just hold the line.

Tom, run to the cottage and call for help." Tom would not know what to do, and he spoke only English. "Forget it. Bang on doors. Bring help. Just a little longer Solveig." Gathering all of his strength, he pulled Sarah fully into the boat. "Sarah. Answer me Sarah. Oh God no. Sarah, Sarah." Fog closed on Daniel's mind. Vaguely aware of many hands and voices, he felt despair so deep that he longed for death.

On either side, strangers were lifting him to a sitting position. "Can you stand?" he heard, so he stood. Fully aware, he searched frantically for Sarah. "Easy now, the girl is in good hands." He looked to the shore and saw two men and a woman in jump suits trotting up the hill with a gurney. On it, bundled and strapped, was Sarah. Following close behind was Tom trying to keep pace. A roar from the hill made it clear—Sarah would be evacuated by air. She must be alive; he dared to consider. Over the din he heard Solveig call to him; he spotted her on the shore wrapped in a blanket.

"Are you all right?" Solveig called to him, and he gave a nod. "Then I must go with them, to Arendal." For the first time in his life, he saw Solveig run.

He declined several offers of coffee, and an invitation to join a couple for dinner. An old man furled the boat's mainsail to the boom, while his wife took down and folded the jib. Little by little, the group dispersed, and though Daniel was used to being alone, he never felt more alone in his life.

Too distressed to work, Daniel walked, and worried, and chastised himself. He feared sleeping; he dreamed of drowning children he could never reach. From Solveig's phone call, he learned that Sarah was recovering, but because of the blow to her head, she would need to be observed closely for at least a week. And no, he need not come to Arendal. Sarah did not want to see him. She was right to blame him. He was responsible. All that kept him on Lyngør was the slim chance that he could offer assistance. At the least, he could offer an admission of guilt. His problems with Birk and Ingrid were nothing in comparison to this. When a week had passed Solveig called to tell him that they were returning; Sarah would still require several weeks of bed rest.

Tom was the first one to leave the water taxi, and when he saw Daniel, he rushed forward; Daniel braced for a blow. Grabbing Daniel by the shoulders he said, "How can I ever thank you. If you hadn't taken charge like you did, Sarah would have . . ." He sniffed. "Thank you." Tom took Daniel by the arm. "Come." And he led Daniel to the seawall, where Solveig was unfolding a wheelchair, and two men were assisting Sarah from the boat.

A bandage covered the left side of Sarah's shaved head. As Daniel approached, he saw a dark cast around her eyes, and scratches on her face. How could he atone for this transgression? It was only right that Tom should mock him.

What a fool he was to meet the boat—it would do Sarah no good to see him. But when her dark eyes met his, she smiled. *Oh Sarah, why?* Tears welled in Daniel's eyes, and he began to sob.

Stunned, and off guard, Daniel was suddenly engulfed by Solveig's arms and perfume. "Our hero," Solveig said in a voice that would have carried to Gjeving. It was a lie. It was because of him that Sarah nearly died. He could never redeem himself, but he could stay out of the way so that Sarah could rest. And if he could find no other way to help, he would leave.

Several hours after the water taxi left, Solveig came to Daniel's apartment. "Sarah is sleeping. Now I want to see how you are doing."

"Can I be of some use? I can use the skiff to get things Sarah might need."

Solveig shook her head. "I must ask you again for a favour. It is very important that Sarah have a quiet place for recovery."

"Naturally, I would do nothing to disturb her."

"Let us sit, and talk a little." They pulled up two chairs, and sat facing each other. Solveig leaned forward and put her hand on Daniel's arm. "I knew you would understand. There is no need to finish this job quickly, and Sarah's recovery is more important." She sighed. "Everything has changed. Tom was to have gone back to America with Sarah a week ago, but who knows how soon she can travel? I should be in Oslo, but of course I will stay here as long as necessary. I hope you understand."

"Yes of course. It will not take long for me to pack."

"What are you saying?"

"I can understand why you did not want me to come to Arendal, and if I leave there will not be a reminder here of my negligence."

Solveig shook his arm. "Listen to me you crazy man. Sarah was sleeping most of the time, and there was no need for a third person to stare at the walls in the visitors' lounge. I did not want to burden you. When I called Ingrid about Sarah, I told her the same thing. Are you listening? And what negligence are you talking about? There was an accident, and you saved the day—everyone knows that."

"I was the teacher. I was the adult taking responsibility. Did I teach her the proper way to leave a boat?"

"She is ten years old. You could have told her one hundred times how to—"

"No, Sarah is not like that. And it was you that jumped in the water. I just stood there."

"Sarah and I might have drowned together if you had not come to our aid." Solveig sighed. "Why are you so anxious to take blame?"

Daniel stood. "I better pack."

Solveig yanked on his arm. "Oh no Daniel Nordal. You

wanted to be of use? You can stay here and at least be company for Sarah. She is very fond of you."

Daniel yielded to the pressure on his arm, and though he sat again, he would not look at Solveig.

"You are carrying too much weight for one person," Solveig said softly. "Let me help? Maybe I have some good news for you. With all this trouble, I neglected to tell you—I talked with my lawyer about your situation. It is complicated. Anna Olsen is probably still a legal citizen of Norway, but if Birk was born in the US, well, he is probably a citizen there, and Norway does not recognize dual citizenships. It will take Birk's lawyers a long time to put everything together to his advantage, if they can. And Lillesand has an interest in seeing that the skerries remain undisturbed." She took a deep breath. "So, according to my friend, this would be a bad business move for Birk. It will cost him a great deal of time and money, and in the end he may not get what he wants."

"Unless he is more stubborn than wise."

"Yes, or his lawyers want to extract as much money from him as possible."

"That would be justice."

"My friend said that the best thing he could do would be to donate the land to the county. Otherwise, there will be a heavy tax liability. Of course, if he just wanted to keep the property in the family for a vacation retreat, it would be easier and less expensive. Whatever happens, it will not happen quickly. Do you feel better?"

"If Birk can find a way to manipulate the system, he will do it."

"If he thinks that way, then he has never done business in Norway. Do not worry Daniel, and do not give your money away to a lawyer."

"I cannot leave anything to chance. As for me—I have nothing to lose."

She slid her chair closer to Daniel. "What am I to do with you?" She waited until he looked at her. "Something happened between you and Ingrid. Would you like to talk about it?"

Daniel shook his head. "Did you know about Ingrid, going to Oslo?"

Solveig laughed. "Everyone in Lillesand knows but you. Is that why—"

"No, no. I do not judge her past."

"You have far too much time on your hands. Let me see if Sarah is awake. Bring her some of those oat crackers with lingonberries she is so fond of. She would like to see you." She slid her chair back. "So you talked with Ingrid about something other than your problems. Good!"

He managed a weak smile. "Talking about my problems has become yet another problem."

"Let us focus on Sarah."

Daniel watched as Sarah, propped on two pillows, gobbled

the crackers he brought. She did not look anything like the healthy girl he knew just a week ago. *What have I done to you?* Trembling legs caused him to lean against the wall to keep from falling. More than anything, he wanted to ask for forgiveness, but he knew he did not deserve it.

"Too bad I'm not Norwegian," Sarah said through a mouth full of crackers. She swallowed what was in her mouth and pointed to her bandaged head. "My father said Norwegians have thick heads."

In spite of his misery, Daniel could not help but laugh, and the laughter lightened his load. "Sarah, this Norwegian's head is very thick."

She picked up another cracker, looked at it, and threw it down. "I really messed things up didn't I?"

Daniel stepped to the head of her bed. "What do you mean Sarah?"

"I'm just a big bother." She pushed the dish of crackers away. "Ingrid didn't want to spend another day teaching a kid. She left because of me. Then I go and bang my head, and now my dad is grumping about missing his trip. And I probably messed up stuff for you too."

Daniel sat on the edge of the bed and took Sarah's hand. "There is nothing you could mess up for me."

"What about Ingrid?"

"Ingrid is very fond of you." He cleared his throat. "She did not leave because of you."

"Then why?"

"It has something to do with me. Not you."

"Do you like Ingrid?"

Daniel's mouth opened to speak, but his jaw hung slack. After a pause, he nodded.

"Is she going to visit us again?"

Daniel shrugged.

"I like her too." She picked at a cracker. "Ingrid's boat is bigger, and it has a wheel."

"So you are thinking of sailing. You are not afraid?"

"Nah" Sarah twisted her face in disgust. "Solveig said you live by yourself on an island." She raised an eyebrow. "Why?"

That he preferred to live alone came to mind, but a part of him knew the answer would be unsatisfactory. Such a complicated matter that he did not fully understand. How could he answer it for this ten-year-old girl? He wanted to change the subject, but before he could think it through, Sarah spoke.

"I know I wouldn't want to live alone."

An image of Linda and Emma crept into his consciousness, bringing a wave of regret and sorrow. He turned his head so Sarah would not see his wet eyes.

"Would you like a cracker?" Sarah asked. As he gazed out of the window, Sarah talked rapidly about the hospital, about school, and about her friends.

Silently, he thanked her for changing the subject, and he forced his reluctant mind to listen to her story.

Daniel sat in the garden, and mulled over Sarah's questions. Before long, Solveig joined him and said, "Daniel, I hope you do not mind. I need someone to talk to."

He could see that her eyes were red, and her cheeks were wet. "Of course. Please sit here."

"I have made such a big mistake," Solveig said. "Yes, Sarah is such a sweet girl, but Tom . . ." She dabbed at her eyes with a handkerchief. "How could I not see it? He is so self-centred. He worries more about being inconvenienced than about Sarah's injury. She cannot travel, so I cannot ask him to leave."

"She travelled all the way from Arendal; surely it would be a much shorter trip to a nice hotel. I would think the water taxi could take them directly to Risør." He realized at once that though his statement was logical, it was not what he wanted.

"Yes, I thought of that too, but you know Tom cannot care for her properly. No, not in her condition." She sucked in a deep breath. "So for Sarah, until she has recovered, I will pretend that nothing has changed." Solveig looked like she just woke from a dream. "Oh, I should not trouble you with my business."

17

The days that followed Sarah's return from the hospital were unbearably long for Daniel. Since there was little that he could do that would not make noise, he visited Sarah often and took long walks, but there were not enough paths and trails on the islands of Lyngør to satisfy his needs. Anxiety and restlessness drove Daniel to make a decision; he would spend the weekend at Lillesand. With Sarah still recovering, it would make Solveig nervous if he stayed away too long, but an overnight trip would do no harm. He would rent a boat, check on the island, and come back the next day. Though expecting that Solveig would argue against the trip, she expressed enthusiasm over his decision and presented a grin that he could not decipher.

Early Saturday morning, Daniel carried his duffle onto the first westbound bus from Gjeving. As there were no direct buses to Lillesand, he would ride for three hours on as many buses with more than enough time to ponder a host of problems. In what condition would he find the cabin? What if Birk were there? Though the purpose of the trip was to check the island, thoughts of Ingrid floated to the surface. After all, he would have to go to the Lillesand marina to rent a boat. How could he avoid her? Would she misunderstand his presence? He had to pull his thinking back to his task, for he was the only one who took Birk seriously. But maybe it would be good to talk with Ingrid, to clear the air. By the time he arrived in Lillesand, Daniel decided that he had a responsibility; he was obliged to give Ingrid a first-hand report on Sarah's recovery.

Though he thought he had packed a light bag, Daniel found the walk to the marina unusually fatiguing, so that he had to use his inhaler. When he reached Ingrid's sloop, he found the sails stowed and the cabin door locked. Either Ingrid went away, Daniel surmised, or she was in Lillesand but had no intention of using the boat that weekend. After walking around the marina and seeing no sign of her Volvo, he went into the office to inquire. Ingrid, he learned, took the day off and would be out of town for the weekend. She had received a call from a girl who had been in an accident in Lyngør, and she went to visit her. He was in no mood for the return walk and bus ride. In any case, he concluded, it was only Sarah that Ingrid wanted to see, so he rented a skiff with a motor.

It felt to Daniel as if the duffle bag contained stone, as he slid it over the gunwale to the island's dock. He dragged the bag a short distance, released the strap, and let the bag lie on the ground as he walked on. After using his inhaler, he pressed ahead up the bluff to the cabin.

What Daniel saw, his mind refused to accept. His legs buckled, and down on his knees he stared in disbelief. Was this the right island? He would look again—give his eyes a second chance. No, there was no doubt, the cabin was gone. Totally destroyed by fire.

While a breeze from the sea moved the ash about in wisps, Daniel rose on shaking legs and looked about. A blackened sink and a couple of pots were the only visible signs that someone had lived there. Kicking up a grey haze, he uncovered a pair of hinges, nails, and one edge of a picture frame that he picked up and examined. The frame once held a picture of Linda and Emma. Daniel kicked at the ash until he was totally engulfed in a cloud of his own making, then he started to bellow, and moan. "Birk, come here damn you. I am waiting for you." He shouted challenge after challenge until his voice failed and tears mixed with the ash.

Then Daniel observed a new shed at the edge of the clearing. It was protected with a sturdy hasp and padlock. He pulled and yanked on the lock until his hands bled, and then he remembered the dream. It was on Lyngør that he had the dream. In that dream, the cabin burned to the ground. In that dream, children played at the cove. *The cove.* What has Birk done at the cove? He smashed his fist against the shed. The fastest way to the cove was by boat, so he stumbled down the trail and flung his bag into the skiff with a strength he did not possess twenty minutes before.

The first thing Daniel noticed were fewer trees at the cove. He gunned the engine and let the boat ride up on the narrow strip of sand. The engine's scream blended with the moan from Daniel's throat, and he sat there transfixed until the smell of hot oil told him the engine was still thrusting. Hoping to find Birk, he jumped from the boat and scanned the cove. Then he realized that he had not observed a boat. Birk would never camp on the island alone.

He found no signs of construction. Not even the beginnings of an excavation. But the birch trees, the trees he loved—gone! The trees that made the cove special. The trees that Linda loved so much. He picked up a freshly cut birch log and struck it again and again against a rock until it was nothing but splinters. Exhausted, he understood that it was well that Birk was gone. He sought the bench, and found it knocked over, intact but badly scraped. So he set it aright, and sat there staring at the water. Daniel struggled to find resolution and release, but he could find no answers, and he could find no more tears.

Without a bedroll or winter coat, he did the best he could by layering what was in the duffle over what he wore. The cold wind drove him to seek refuge in the lee of a boulder, but the wind shifted and penetrated his shelter. There was nothing to do but pace and shiver. As he paced along the shore in the moonlight his rage grew, and his desire for revenge became an obsession. By the time the black sky turned blue, he knew what to do.

After grabbing the gas can from the skiff, Daniel rushed along the trail to the cabin site. With hands shaking, he splashed gasoline over the locked shed. Remembering a discarded cigarette lighter, he rummaged in the ash until he found it. It was out of fuel, but all he needed was a spark from the striker. He stood back from the shed, but close enough so he could lean forward and reach it with the lighter. He flicked the striker; at once light and heat blasted his face. Then a roar and a growing brilliance of light. Daniel pulled back sharply. As the shed broke up, he could see shovels, picks, a crowbar, rolled sheets of paper, surveyors tape, stakes, and a sledge-hammer. While he watched, and warmed himself, he felt a growing pain in his hand. The hand he used to start the fire. It looked red and swollen, so he climbed down the bluff to the shore and thrust his hand in water.

Though the fire was burning out, Daniel saw a thick column of smoke rise from the cabin site. That was sure to bring any passing boater in close for a look. It was time to leave. As he walked back to the cove, sadness gradually replaced satisfaction, and he began to wonder if he was becoming like Birk. Stress and sleeplessness had sapped his energy; he could barely put one foot in front of the other.

A flood of new questions came to mind. Should he have checked with the county authorities first? If the property title were unchanged, then maybe Birk would have been fined or worse. Nevertheless, Birk would certainly have needed a special permit to burn the cabin. How could he make a report now that he destroyed property as well? What if the fire at the cabin had been an accident? Perhaps Birk had nothing to do with it.

Just before he reached the cove, a woman called his name. It was felt more than heard, and he remembered the last time it happened—the morning he learned of Birk. *Linda?* No, what was he saying? It was just exhaustion. But the presence grew, and the message became clear. *Go home Daniel.* Then he emerged at the cove, and he knew he was alone again. Home? Where is home? Ingrid had asked that question, he remembered. Still, he could not answer.

He wrestled the boat into the water, and was relieved when the motor coughed and roared.

With the infrequency of Sunday buses, it was evening by the time Daniel arrived at Lyngør. All he wanted to do was sleep, and if possible, forget. Within five minutes of entering the apartment, Solveig was at the door. "My God, what has happened to you," she said with alarm. She gasped, and her hands flew to her mouth. "Have you looked at yourself?"

He stepped back, and Solveig followed him into the room. The reflection in the window revealed a stranger with soot on his face that had become streaked and caked under the eyes. The tangle that was Daniel's hair had become ash grey.

"I camped on the island, and built a fire to keep warm. I guess some of the soot must have blown on me." He forced a laugh. "So that is why people at the bus terminal at Arendal moved away from me. I should have brought a mirror in my bag." He yawned. "It has been a long day. Bad bus connections. You know how it is."

She folded her arms and stepped closer to him. "I suppose you used yourself for kindling. If I am your friend, you will tell me the truth or tell me to mind my own business. Either way is fine. Come in the back, and sit down before you fall down. God, what happened to your hand?"

"Just a little burn," Daniel mumbled.

"Wash it while I get some salve from my apartment."

As he stood at the sink, he considered telling Solveig everything. It would be good to share some of his burden. Burning the shed was most certainly against the law. Would the police come looking for him? Of course, she would not report him, but it would not be fair to involve her. Maybe she would ask him to leave. Oh God, what if Sarah should see him taken away by the police. Was Linda really there? She could have helped him act reasonably. She always did. He would only need for her to talk with him—to calm him. He felt a touch on his arm.

"Dry yourself and come sit at the table." Solveig handed him a towel, and unscrewed the cap of a tube. After they sat, she gently rubbed ointment on his hand. "So, do you want to tell me?"

"Maybe later, when things change." He was surprised to find tears welling, and he wondered if things would ever change, and he regretted saying it, and he knew at that moment that Solveig would ask, What things?

"That is good enough for me," Solveig said softly. "Did you know that Ingrid was here?"

"It was kind of her to visit with Sarah."

"Yes, Sarah is something." She shook her head. "She took it on herself to call Ingrid and ask her to come." Solveig laughed. She capped the ointment, and her smile faded. "I wish Sarah had told me. Maybe you would have stayed here." She sighed and went to the sink to wash her hands. "Sarah was disappointed that you were not here," she said over her shoulder. "I think Ingrid was disappointed too."

"No, Ingrid came to see Sarah, not me."

Solveig shook her head. "Oh Daniel." She came back to the table and started to speak, but stopped abruptly. "Never mind. Let me get away so you can sleep. This is not a good time."

Still sitting at the table; too weary to bathe or even to stand, Daniel dropped his ash-covered head on his arms. One thought passed through his mind before his awareness faded. *Go home, Daniel.*

18

Sarah sat in bed supported by, in Daniel's estimation, every pillow in Lyngør. She scowled and asked, "Why did you have to go back to that stupid island?"

"Do you wonder if your house is okay? If your room is unchanged while you are away?" Sarah continued to scowl, so Daniel offered her a cracker. "Here, I brought your favourite." She refused to take one, so he placed the plate on her bedside stand.

"Solveig said it's not even yours. Don't you live *here* now?"

"There was another reason Sarah. I wanted to tell Ingrid how well you were doing."

She frowned, and her voice became barely audible. "You could have just called. You could have asked her to visit." She folded her arms. "Ingrid was here."

"I did not know until I reached Lillesand."

"Suppose I told you? Would you have stayed?"

"Did you have a nice visit?" He watched her frown deepen. "Can I get you something else to eat?"

Sarah unfolded her arms and pushed the cracker plate as far away as possible. "I don't like islands, and I can't wait to go."

"But it is very peaceful here. I think you will miss it when you leave."

She let herself fall back against the pillows. "Maybe if there were friends and stuff to do."

Daniel felt his stomach tighten. She does not consider me a friend, he considered. Perhaps she has come to blame me after all. "Friends are important," he said hesitantly.

"Then why do you live alone?"

"Maybe not anymore." He could not believe what he said.

"Good!" She smiled and leaned forward. "What about Ingrid?"

"Ah, so that is what this is all about." He laughed and felt relieved. "Things are not so simple."

"Yes they are." She stretched over the bedside stand to fetch the crackers.

He said goodbye and promised to visit with her soon. As he was leaving her room, he thought of the old saying, *drunks and children tell the truth.*

Daniel found Solveig in the garden, and said, "It seems that Sarah is trying to be—"

"Matchmaker?" Solveig winked. "Yes, I was in the next room while you were talking with her. She is very fond of both of you and naturally would like to see you together. And, right now, she has nothing better to do. But I was not there to eavesdrop; there is something important I have to tell you. Daniel, a stranger has been asking for you."

It must be the police, he decided, and his stomach churned. All he needed was five minutes to gather his belongings and pile them in the skiff, but they would expect him to leave by water. Wasn't there a rocky and wooded area on the windward side of Odden? He should have made a plan. "Where is he?"

"He was asking questions at the post office." She cocked her head. "Are you okay? Is this about that weekend in Lillesand?"

"At the post office? No, nobody knows me."

"Yes they do. Since Sarah's accident, everybody knows about you. But this man has passed word that he wants to meet you at noon, at The Blue Lantern."

"How strange. A policeman who wants to invite me to a restaurant."

"Oh my God. Police? Now you must tell me all about it."

No, the police would not act this way. Momentarily relieved, Daniel considered alternatives. Birk? Of course, the coward would want to talk in a public place. But why?

"Daniel?"

"Maybe it is best to tell you." They strolled along the shore of Odden while Daniel told her almost everything that happened that weekend. It was a relief to relate the account to

Solveig, but at the same time, he felt a sense of shame. "I believe the man who wants to meet me is Birk Olsen."

"You should go away Daniel. Just for a little while. If he provokes you, then you will only hurt yourself in the end. Remember what happened at the island with your anger"

"I was surprised by what I saw, and I reacted. But now, I can prepare myself. A part of me wants to leave, but I am weary Solveig. It is time to end this business. I will go and see Birk or whoever is there." They stopped at the end of the shore path. "You have been a good friend." He startled Solveig by giving her a hug.

It was an hour before noon; he wanted to think, so he walked. He envisioned that people would shun him when they learned the truth. Ingrid would think him unstable, and Sarah would fear him. Once Solveig had time to think about it, she would not want an arsonist working in her shop. He imagined Birk sneering as he was led away to jail. But what about principle? Was he not honouring Ole and Anna Olsen who wanted their land protected? Was he not honouring the memory of his wife and daughter? Why should the law care about his integrity? Honour is more important than law. He clung to that thought, but his grip felt weak.

Daniel came to a ridge on Holmen that provided a view of the mainland. Sitting on a slab of stone, he tried to free his mind from fear. If only he could be at the cove then perhaps Linda's presence would come. She could help him. He rebuked himself for such nonsense, but still, it might help to pretend. After looking, to be certain he was alone, he began to speak to Linda of all his doubts and fears. Daniel spoke about the island and his conflict with Birk, and his guilt over Sarah's injury, and even about his night with Ingrid. It was as if she were there; he could imagine her sitting by his side. She listened with compassion in her eyes, and she took his hand. As he spoke, he began to understand—his problems were in the past, and his fears were intangible—today was just today and nothing more. With a newfound lightness, he jumped to his feet. It was time for his meeting. Daniel felt at peace.

As he walked down the hill, he tried unsuccessfully to recover Linda's image. By the time The Blue Lantern came into view, doubts began to seep into his consciousness. Did he just talk to a ghost? Was he losing his mind? Was this the result of living alone too long?

A man stood, leaning on the rail, alone on the restaurant's deck. His back was to Daniel, and he was looking out over the Sound. The elfin ears poking up along the sides of the watch cap were unmistakable; it was Eric who asked for the meeting. Was he bringing a threat from Birk, or was he here as a friend with a warning?

Eric's body stiffened as Daniel's feet struck the deck, and he did not turn as Daniel came closer. "Hello Daniel, thank you for meeting me."

Daniel joined Eric at the railing, but Eric still kept his gaze on the water. "What do you see out there?" Daniel asked.

"Another time, a busy village, wooden ships under sail." Eric smiled and turned to shake Daniel's hand. "What happened to your hand?"

"An old burn that is healing. You would rather be out there?" Daniel nodded toward the sea.

"For a seaman, the sea always calls." His eyes swept the horizon. "Sometimes the sea is terrible, and unforgiving. Fools and dreamers long to be out there."

"You are certainly not a fool Eric Haugen."

Eric laughed. "And I am too old to dream, but you are not. What do you dream of?" When Daniel did not reply, Eric said, "I see that you have found another island."

"I have a job here." What a strange meeting, Daniel thought. The anxiety of the morning had dissolved, and he was glad to see Eric again.

"Please excuse my curiosity, but would you have taken a job on the mainland?"

A shiver went through Daniel. "Come inside. We can talk over coffee." He turned away from the railing while pondering Eric's question. The question made him uncomfortable, and he could find no answer. Eric followed him to a corner table with a view of the Sound, and they ordered coffee.

"You could have asked where I was living. Why did you want me to meet you here?" Daniel asked.

"I am an intruder. You should be able to choose to meet me or not."

"You would never be an intruder. You saved my life."

"Forgive me, but you seem to find satisfaction in isolation. Or do you? Would you always want to live on your island near Lillesand?"

A variety of routine responses floated in Daniel's head. Peace and quiet. Comfort in routine. Yes, and he was faithful to the memory of his family. But when Daniel opened his mouth, he said, "No."

Eric put his coffee mug down and looked at Daniel with tired eyes. "When I was a young man, I took a job as a deck hand on a bulk carrier on the west coast. With me was a young man from my hometown. We grew up together, and dreamed of having our own ship. One day as we rounded the coast near Fløro, we were caught in a terrible storm and the ship was driven aground. My friend was trapped below deck when the ship broke up." Eric took a deep breath. "He lost his life that day. I never sailed in a bulk carrier again. I even turned down jobs in other coastal vessels." Eric shook his head. "I never went near Fløro again."

Daniel turned to look at the Sound. "If you were me, you would have left the island forever. You would have gone home to—"

"No, I do not know what I would have done. I did not come here to tell you what to do."

Daniel sipped from his mug. "Have you seen Birk?"

"I quit working for him shortly after you left." Eric looked closely at Daniel's burned hand. "From the island fire?"

"You know?"

Eric laughed. "Everyone in Lillesand knows, and of course I thought about you. I remembered Ingrid Larsen, a friend of yours, at the marina. So, I asked her if you were still here."

"Then I am wanted by the police."

"I doubt it. There was some curiosity about a small fire reported in the skerries. Probably some students having a party and being careless. It has already been forgotten." Eric shrugged. "I remember reading that the police could not reach the landowner. It is probable that no one has been accused."

"Did you come here to find out if I did it?"

Eric took out his pipe and examined it. "I am not sure why I came. I have to admire a man with such strong loyalty to his family. And, I am curious about a man who will fight to live alone. Maybe it is the seaman in me, but when another man seems to be drowning one cannot sit by."

Daniel felt his eyes moisten. "Now that you see me, do you think I am drowning?" He watched as Eric pondered his question, and it seemed to Daniel that Eric looked older than he remembered.

"I am not so sure now. Maybe you have found yourself a life jacket here on Lyngør. But you know, I did not come to pry into your life. I offer you a hand, if you want it."

Daniel could find no suitable words, so he simply nodded.

Eric smiled, and brought his pipe to his forehead in salute. "I have too little time." He looked at his watch. "Would you like to show me your work?" They stood, and Eric took Daniel's good hand in both of his, and with a firm grip, shook his hand.

When they came to the post office, they saw Solveig pacing by the entrance. When she saw the two men approach, she turned to the bulletin board and studied the notices that had not been changed in months. When Daniel came near he said, "Nothing to worry about, Solveig." She let out a breath that she clearly had been holding, and her face relaxed. "Come with us. Have you met my friend Eric?"

Eric looked at the work Daniel had completed. "I could never do work like that," Eric said, and he talked about his limited experiences with woodworking. Then they went to the garden and joined Solveig, and in a sheltered corner—in a lawn chair, wrapped in a blanket—was Sarah.

"Ah, here is Sarah. We must talk English now," Daniel said.

Solveig shrugged. "She fussed until I brought her outside."

Sarah put down the book that she had held in front of her face. "If I had to spend one more day in that room I'd die."

"I would feel the same way," Daniel said. "You must be doing better." He introduced Sarah to Eric. Then turning to Eric he said, "Maybe she is one of my life jackets now. She is a very wise young lady."

Sarah wrinkled her nose. "I'm not a life jacket. Don't you mean I should have worn one?"

"That too Sarah."

"Daniel saved Sarah's life," Solveig said. She went on to explain the events of Sarah's accident.

"Oh no," Daniel said. "All of us worked together." He felt Eric's hand on his shoulder. "Do not forget how the people of Lyngør worked together, and how fast the rescue service came." And do not forget who was responsible, he thought.

"You protest too much," Solveig said.

"I have enjoyed meeting all of you," Eric said, "but sadly, if I do not catch the next ferry I will not be able to get a bus." Daniel asked him to stay another day, and offered lodging, which he declined. Eric brushed off Daniel's offer to walk with him to the ferry. They promised to talk again soon, and Eric walked away while whistling an old folk tune that Daniel recognized. It was about a weary traveller who longed for home.

"Is he a friend of yours?" asked Sarah.

"Yes, and now I realize how fortunate I am with such good friends as you and Solveig." It occurred to him that he omitted Tom. "And your father of course." He saw in her eyes that she noted the omission. Seeking to cover his blunder, he added, "Oh, and of course Ingrid." She brought the book up to cover her face.

"Where is Tom?" Daniel asked Solveig in a low voice.

She shrugged and rolled her eyes. "Since Sarah is doing better, if you want to start work again it would be okay. But it would be best, for her sake, if you do not start before eight in the morning."

Happy to be working again, Daniel started work at exactly eight the following day. After making an estimate of what was required to complete the project, he decided that he would be finished in two weeks.

Later that day, Tom appeared and took Sarah away in the water taxi. Solveig said it was for a clinic appointment to check her progress. When they returned, Sarah was free of her bandage, and Tom reported that there was no need for additional medical visits. They were free to travel as they wished.

Solveig set Sarah up with her book in the garden, but as soon as Solveig went inside, Daniel saw her throw her book to the ground. So he set aside his work and went to the garden to join her. Her chin was on her chest, and she did not stir when he approached. "Can I get you some crackers with lingonberries?" She did not answer, but stared straight ahead. "Sarah, are you okay?" He saw her blink. He took another chair and set it next to hers. They sat together without speaking for five minutes. When she finally looked at him, he asked, "Would you like to talk?"

She folded her arms and pouted. "I don't want to leave."

"Did someone say you were leaving?"

"The doctor told my dad that it was okay to go. My father wants to leave as soon as he can—next week."

"I am so glad that you are doing well. I will miss you Sarah. Do you remember not long ago, you said you wanted to leave?"

"Now I don't want to go. I want to go sailing again with you and Ingrid."

"The weather is turning cold, and it will not be so much fun on the water. Maybe your father will bring you to Norway next summer. I promise you all the sailing time you want when you come back."

She turned her head away from him.

"I have an idea. We will have a big party before you leave."

Sarah remained quiet for a time, but she turned back to face him and a smile crept up one corner of her mouth. "I'll invite Ingrid," she said firmly.

"I should ask Solveig and your father about the party first."

She started to unbundle herself. "I'll call Ingrid right now."

19

Sarah was going home, and Daniel felt an ache in his soul. There were very few people he had felt close to in his life. His parents and his own family had died, he had alienated Ingrid, and now Sarah would go away—probably forever. Of course, she had to leave; Norway was not her home. There was nothing he could do but to let his work engulf him. Remaining alone on Lyngør was not a choice he cared to make; he decided to finish the project in a week. As staining and varnishing wood did not create noise, he planned to work late every night. No sooner had he launched his plan, than Solveig came to the shop.

"That is a wonderful idea to have a party for Sarah. The idea has certainly lifted her spirits. Do you have a minute?" Solveig held her nose. "Paint fumes bother me. Can we step outside?" Daniel nodded and followed her into the garden.

"The plan is," Solveig said excitedly, "that they will leave here in the evening a week from today. They will take the SAS flight from Kristiansand to Copenhagen and from there they will fly to New York. The flight is Friday morning, so they will need to spend Thursday night near the airport." She paused for a deep breath. "At first I thought we should have the party on the weekend, but then Sarah called Ingrid."

Daniel waited for an explanation, but then he realized that Solveig was waiting for a reaction. "Sarah told me she would call."

Solveig smiled. "Ingrid will come here on Wednesday with her boat and Sarah can ride on the sloop to Gjeving. They would have to go by boat anyway, but this will be special for her. A farewell sailing!"

"This is very generous of Ingrid."

"I invited Ingrid to stay here Thursday night." She studied Daniel's face. "Are you pleased?"

"Now that the days are shorter, it would be too late to sail back to Lillesand that same evening."

The varnish on the counter in Solveig's shop was still wet on the day of Sarah's departure. It had been a busy week. The only break he took was for a trip to Risør to buy presents for Sarah and Tom. All of his belongings were packed and the apartment was clean. Lillesand was where he wanted to go, but he had been too busy to make a plan.

By noon, all preparations were complete; it was almost time for Ingrid to arrive. Sarah paced along the shore, and asked Daniel repeatedly, "Can you see the boat yet?"

"No Sarah. Remember she cannot do more than the wind

or her boat will allow. But, if any sailor can be on time, Ingrid can."

Sarah turned away. "She promised once before."

"Ingrid will come." Oh please Ingrid, Daniel thought, and his stomach started to ache. "See if Solveig has some oats for the swan."

Suddenly Sarah whooped and shouted for Solveig and Tom, who came running from the cottage. "Ingrid is here. See?" She pointed to a boat rounding Outer Lyngør.

"It is too far," Daniel said cautiously.

"Sarah has the eyes of a hawk," Tom said.

Daniel could see the boat had the lines of Ingrid's sloop, and then he could see coloured streamers running from the rigging. It must be Ingrid. Solveig fumbled with a camera that still had a tag on it, and Sarah leaned toward the boat as if that act would bring it closer. Then, as the boat approached, there was absolute certainty; they could see Ingrid. "Come quick, everyone to the dock," Daniel said, and everyone started to run.

Ingrid brought the boat smartly about so that the stern passed in view of the group. Just then, Sarah began to bawl.

"What happened?" Solveig asked Daniel in a whisper.

"Ingrid had never given her boat a name, but as you can see . . ." He pointed to the passing stern. In fresh gold paint was the name *SARAH*.

In a blur of movement, with one hand on the wheel, Ingrid set the jib free, dropped the main, and came to within arms reach alongside the dock. And there was no shortage of eager hands to secure the sloop.

The weather was fair, so they held the party in the garden. Solveig had arranged for a Lyngør resident, skilled in the Hardanger fiddle, to play at the party. He taught them a folk dance, and when they could dance no longer, he taught them old songs that they sang with gusto. Laughter echoed across Lyngør Sound. Through it all, Daniel and Ingrid never exchanged a word.

When the shadows grew long, they gathered around a table that Solveig had set with cake, waffles with berries, cookies, and ice cream. When everyone ate their fill, Solveig announced that it was time for everyone to go to the upstairs apartment. There would be a surprise for Sarah.

Solveig presented Sarah with the new camera that she had used when Ingrid arrived. It contained pictures of the sloop *Sarah*, and scenes from the party. Ingrid gave her a small wooden box, hand decorated with rosmaling, and inside the lid was a painting of sunrise at Lyngør. Each presentation drew a squeal from Sarah, quickly followed by a hug.

Daniel asked Tom to step forward, and presented him with a piece of luggage. "Please note on the tag that this piece is guaranteed to be water resistant. I have not tested it, but I believe it will float if dropped in the Sound." Everyone except Sarah laughed. Tom made a show of inspecting the seams; he nodded approval and patted Daniel on the back. "Now if Sarah will come here?" He watched Sarah's expression progress from frown, to surprise, to delight.

Daniel's hand trembled, as he presented her with a small box made of walnut. Its hinge and latch were of gleaming brass. Eagerly, she flipped the top back to uncover a fitted case containing a brass compass. The inside of the lid contained an inscribed plate that Sarah read aloud.

For Sarah,
a fine sailor, who has taught me much.
Daniel Nordal
Lyngør Norway, September 4, 1996

Her voice slowed when she read the second line. Daniel feared that she would ask about the meaning, but she continued reading as Solveig and Ingrid exchanged glances. The expected squeal did not come. Sarah stared without expression at the compass while Daniel cursed himself for his foolish choice. What in God's name would a ten-year-old girl want with a boat's compass? Then all at once, Sarah was on him, and he was awash with tears and hugs. Through his blurred vision, he was certain that Ingrid cried too.

Standing together at the seawall, Solveig and Daniel watched the sloop *Sarah* sail toward Gjeving. They saw Ingrid turn the wheel over to Sarah, and with one hand on the wheel, Sarah turned and waved to them.

The evening air became chilly as the sloop disappeared behind Holmen. "I wonder if we will ever see her again," Daniel said.

Solveig sighed and wiped at her eyes. "In my heart, I think we will not."

"I had better clean up the garden," Daniel said. "I should be finished before Ingrid comes back."

"She will not be back Daniel. Please forgive me for not telling you sooner, but you seemed to be enjoying yourself."

"Why?"

"She told me in a few words during the party. That was not a good time to ask questions."

Daniel shivered. "The wind is picking up; I better pick up the papers in the garden before they blow away." He turned to go back to the garden. "It would be dark along the coast if she sails for Lillesand now."

"No I think she will wait for morning. Ingrid mentioned there was someone she knew at Gjeving." Solveig looked closely at Daniel. "Are you going there?"

The idea lodged in Daniel's mind like a fish bone in his throat. He looked toward Gjeving for a minute. "When I finish here I am going to bed."

The next morning Daniel gathered up the empty paint and varnish cans for disposal. After surveying his work, he felt comfortable that he had done a good job. Solveig would need an electrician, but he could do no more; he would leave that morning.

Solveig prepared a lavish breakfast for him, and with tears in her eyes, she presented him with a hand-knitted sweater in the Setesdal pattern. They pushed money back and forth across the table, as he claimed she paid him too much. To end the matter, Solveig agreed to a lesser sum "for now, but I will settle this later—you can be sure." She offered him the use of the apartment for the winter, but he declined.

"I must go to Oslo at once," Solveig said. "My business has been neglected too long. Would you mind waiting until I finish packing?"

"Certainly, you will need help with your luggage."

"No, I have arranged for a water taxi to come right to the cottage." She shook her head. "Yes, I should have done that when I first arrived with Tom. But Daniel, I want you to stay because I do not want to be here alone. Not for one minute. It must be hard for you to understand." She cleared her throat. "There will be a rental car waiting in Gjeving. I can drive you to Lillesand."

"Lillesand is in the opposite direction from where you are going. You are very kind, but the bus will suit me fine." Daniel glanced out of the window and thought he saw—though it was hard to tell because of the distance and the glare of the morning sun—the sloop *Sarah* skirting Outer Lyngør with two people in the stern.

As the bus closed the distance to Lillesand, Daniel wondered if he truly had a friend in Norway. It was obvious that he had done something to alienate Ingrid. He could always count on her friendship, even though she fussed a lot, but now he felt very alone. What a fool he was to take her for granted. But what about their night together? There seemed to be no answer. Solveig was kind and generous, but she lived in a different world. Eric, on the other hand, was easy to talk with, and he seemed to have an abundance of wisdom to share.

Unable to find Eric at the harbour, Daniel's thoughts turned to food and coffee. At Knudsen's, Greta went automatically for the raisin rolls. It felt good to be remembered, even for such a small thing. But this day he would give Greta something to talk about. He ordered a sandwich with Jarlsberg cheese. At his usual table, Daniel peeled cheese from the edges of his sandwich, and contemplated the future.

After a restful night's sleep at The Kettle, and a morning visit to the bakery, he returned to the harbour and sat on the bench where Eric always sat. After two hours alone in the cold, he walked away, and decided he would try to talk with Ingrid. He would ask her to put aside the night they shared on Lyngør, and restore the friendship they had. The sloop *Sarah* was missing from its berth, so he inquired at the office. Ingrid had several days off, and would not return until Monday.

Several stores were still open on Strandgata so he purchased a sleeping bag and foul weather gear. At a grocer, he bought bread, cheese, tins of mackerel, ground coffee, matches, and several gallons of bottled water. Then he arranged for a water taxi to take him to the island, and to pick him up in three days. In three days he would decide. Either he would oppose Birk Olsen with all his strength, or he would leave the island forever.

Everything at the cabin site was as he left it. Nothing had been salvaged from the burned shed, and there were no footprints in the ash other than his own. It took several trips to bring his supplies from the dock to the cove, and on the last trip, he retrieved the coffee pot from the ashes of the cabin. Noting that the pot looked the same as it did before the fire, caused Daniel to laugh aloud. Perhaps his coffee would gain some extra character. In spite of the cold wind, he was able to make a comfortable camp.

All through the first day, and long into the night, Daniel struggled to reach a decision. He tried talking aloud, and a part of him hoped to hear Linda respond. But—he came to realize—he was totally on his own. Linda was gone, of course, but why could he not move on? In one minute, he wondered why he was fussing over a bunch of logs that were not his. In another, he was determined not to let Birk develop the island. In one minute, he worried about the consequences of his actions. In another, he concluded that he had nothing left to lose. Birk was the enemy. Birk was not worth his time. The island was everything. The island was just an island. On the morning of the second day, he knew what he had to do.

It started to rain. By late morning, the shower became a deluge, and runoff from the hill swamped his camp. Though his foul weather gear kept him comfortable, he found it difficult to prepare food. Rain in his coffee put him in a foul mood. He decided to move to the cabin site where the drainage was better, and where there were suitable trees for rigging a tarp. It took two trips, but he reasoned he would have to do it eventually to reload his gear for the water taxi.

It was noon before he managed a crude shelter, and he was in a position to view a small wedge of the sea. Through the squall, he could make out the form of a sloop coming directly at the island at full speed. Only Ingrid would have that much confidence, but it was not like her to push the limit. Before he could weigh the situation, the sloop was spilling air, and it came against the dock without a fender. The crack brought him to his feet and he slid down the bluff just in time to catch a line. Ingrid jumped from the boat and threw her arms around his neck as though downing, and Daniel felt her body heave with sobs.

"Thank God you are here. Tom said you went back to Lillesand." She had to shout over the noise of the wind and the cacophony of sound that came from the sloop. With their sheets set free, the sails whipped and snapped in the wind, while the fitting on a loose halyard beat against the mast.

"Let me help you secure the boat."

She pushed away from him. "No, leave it alone."

"The sails will—"

She beat against his chest. "Shut up." She wept, and Daniel put his arms around her. "I need you to come with me to Kristiansand. I cannot do it alone." She buried her face against his chest.

Kristiansand? That was where Sarah and Tom went to get a flight, he remembered. Daniel felt a moan rise in his throat, and he forced himself to ask. "Sarah?"

"She is in intensive care."

"An accident?"

"Sarah collapsed at the airport. Tom says they think it was from her head injury at Lyngør."

Hours later, Daniel would wonder if it was the wind, but standing there with Ingrid in his arms—as their tears merged with the rain—he clearly heard, *Go with her Daniel. Go now.*

20

When Ingrid and Daniel arrived at the hospital, they found Tom sitting in the visitor's lounge staring at a two-day-old Norwegian newspaper. Daniel was certain he had never seen someone look as alone as Tom did at that moment.

They exchanged hugs and Tom thanked them for coming. Sarah was unable to have visitors, so they settled down uneasily on the well-worn furniture and listened to Tom's account.

"It's not yet clear what happened—there are still tests to do." Tom took a deep breath. "She is unconscious. They say there may be too much pressure on her brain."

"She will get good care here," Ingrid said. "Thank God this did not happen while you were in the air."

"She seemed all right when we got to the airport. Sarah was self-conscious about the shaved place on her head and the scar, so she wanted to look for a hat at the airport shops. The more we looked, the more irritable she got. Now I think it was more than finding the right hat that made her so cranky. When our flight was announced, Sarah said she had to use the woman's room. She was in there a long time, and when she came out her face was pale. I asked her if she felt sick, but she ignored me." Tom shook his head. "I tried to hurry her to the gate, but she stumbled and said that everything looked fuzzy. Then she put her hands to her head and she screamed. God, she screamed." Tom muffled a sob, and took a deep breath. "Someone called security. Then everything became confused. Before I knew it, we were in an ambulance, and everyone was speaking Norwegian to each other, and as soon as they arrived here they rushed her to intensive care. Finally, someone told me about the pressure on her brain."

"Does Solveig know?" Ingrid asked.

"She had already left Oslo for New York on a business trip. Her manager in Oslo said Solveig would call soon, and she would give her my message."

What could Daniel say or do? This was his doing. How could he possibly redeem himself? He felt ill and wished he could change places with Sarah. He would give anything if that were possible. Looking around, he saw Tom staring at his shoes, and Ingrid staring at an art reproduction that did not deserve such undivided attention. The silence intensified his pain, and the silence stretched on until the sun set.

Ingrid broke the uneasy silence. "It seems there is nothing we can do this evening, so I will return in the morning. Please call if there is any news." She turned to Daniel. "Do you want a ride to Lillesand?"

Daniel looked and saw his own pain reflected in Tom's eyes. How could he leave this man alone with this terrible burden? This man, a stranger in a land that was not his own. "No, I will spend the night here."

Ingrid appeared as if she were going to speak, but changed her mind. She gave Tom and Daniel a hug and wiped her eyes as she left the room.

"I hope you're not staying on my account," Tom said. "You can still catch up with Ingrid."

"Of course I will stay with you, and I want to be here when Sarah wakes up." He thought about the rain, and the make-shift shelter on the island. "Actually, I will be very comfortable here." Daniel shifted his chair, so that he could face Tom. "I guess Solveig has told you something of my life. You must think I am very strange."

Tom raised his hand in protest. "No, I don't think that at all."

"You are very gracious, but I am a strange man. Just a short time ago, I was sitting alone in the rain plotting to challenge a man over a piece of rock and dirt. It seemed very important then, but now . . ."

"We can't see what's important until we're face to face with tragedy. Why is that?"

Daniel wondered if he had learned anything from all his loss. "You are asking a blind man Tom." How much tragedy does it take? *Damn the island.* "I will never forgive myself."

"What are you going on about? Sarah loved sailing." Tom buried his face in his hands. "And what have I done? Her own father." His chest heaved. "Oh God, give me a second chance."

Yes, Daniel thought, give us both a second chance.

"I want to thank you for bringing a smile to my daughter's face. It's something I haven't seen in a long time. And that compass you gave her. I could not pack it or take it away from her. It rode with her on the gurney. On the way to the airport, she went on and on about how she would have a sailboat of her own some day and she would use the compass to find Norway." Tom's eyes brimmed with tears. "You were very kind to her." He grabbed a fistful of tissues from a dispenser on the table. "It's going to be a long night my friend; let's see if we can find some coffee."

They talked and napped intermittently through the night. Tom was allowed a brief visit with Sarah. "She didn't know I was there. There's no change," Tom reported. After breakfast, Ingrid returned; she appeared to have had a sleepless night. Tom was paged, and when he returned, he reported that Solveig had called from New York. Through the morning, they spoke little, and paced often. Then a nurse called Tom away while Daniel and Ingrid sat silently together. After fifteen minutes, Tom returned with a lively step and a smile on his face.

"She recognized me," Tom said as soon as he was in calling distance. Ingrid and Daniel rushed to him and expressed their joy and relief. "You can visit with her one at a time, but only for a few minutes. She must not get excited." Ingrid went first, and when she returned she was sobbing, and motioned for Daniel to go.

It was more than his spirit could stand. There was no doubt; at that moment, he would have given his life to spare her from this. No one could be as vulnerable as Sarah was then. Her eyes were barely visible behind the swollen and blackened patches that circled them. Like a gruesome turban, her head was wrapped in a stained bandage from which a thin tube emerged. Other tubes ran to her arms, and into her nose, and machines on both sides of her bed flashed numbers, and drew serpentine lines on little screens.

Leaning closer to her, he could see that her eyes followed his movement. He came close to the head of the bed and took her cold hand in his, and he forced a smile on his face. "Hello Sarah," he said in a hoarse voice, and he felt her hand gently squeeze his. Sarah's mouth moved, but only spittle emerged, so he leaned to bring his ear close to her mouth. She made barely audible sounds. One of the words sounded like *Ingrid*, but Daniel could not be sure. Fear of stressing her prevented him from asking her to repeat it.

Someone tapped on his shoulder; he turned to see a woman in scrubs gesturing for him to leave. He kissed Sarah's cheek and told her that he would return. The beginning of a smile seemed to be forming in the corner of her mouth. Then her eyes looked to the bedside stand. Daniel followed her gaze and saw the open walnut box with the compass he gave her. The compass card, influenced by a magnetic field in the room, was spinning out of control. Lifting the box, he tried different positions and orientations, but still the card spun. The points of the compass were everywhere, and nowhere, as if relative direction had been suspended. Then another tap on his shoulder. Can it be two minutes already? Is something wrong? What was Sarah trying to tell me?

Too distressed to talk with anyone, Daniel bypassed the visitor's lounge, and left the hospital. More than anything, he needed air; he needed to walk, so as fast as his legs would move he circled the hospital building. Though Sarah was doing better, in his heart he felt that something was terribly wrong. Why should the compass bother him so? Of course, there must be a rational explanation—some equipment in the room. Still, it seemed as if some fundamental order of the world had been disturbed. Then, for a reason he could not fathom, Daniel began to cry. He walked until he became too fatigued to continue, and he slumped into a chair in the hospital lobby.

Tom had another chance to visit Sarah just before noon. Daniel found the silence between Ingrid and himself to be unbearable, so he spoke the first thing that came to mind. "Sarah tried to say something to me. Did she talk to you?"

"She spoke a little, but it seemed to upset her, so I asked her to rest. I promised her I would talk with her later."

"Did you see the compass?"

Ingrid raised an eyebrow and shook her head. Without looking at him, she said, "I think we need to talk about us."

"Yes, I would like that." He looked around. "Perhaps we can find a quiet place outside."

"You must have wondered what happened to me at Lyngør," Ingrid said. "I was rude and unkind; I hope you can forgive me. You did not do anything Daniel. It was not you, it was me. I have always liked you. I was lonely and I followed my heart, but in the morning—I followed my head. We have known each other for years, and I care deeply for you. But . . ." Ingrid turned her head away and sniffed.

"Let me help. I am unpredictable, I live like a hermit, I cling to the past, and I seek out dragons to slay. There is much more. Yes?"

She turned back to him, and tears streamed down her face. "I did not want to hurt you. We should have talked that morning, but I was such a coward."

He took her hand. "I know all about being a coward, for I am the worst kind—I run from myself daily. Oh Ingrid, will you still be my friend?" They threw their arms around each other, and cried together.

Trembling, Ingrid pushed back from him. "There is

something else I have to tell you. After Sarah's party, I stayed in Gjeving. A man I used to work with—"

"You do not have to tell me."

"Yes I do. He invited me to stay overnight. It was foolish of me."

A part of Daniel wanted to say something to ease her burden. To acknowledge her right to choose and to disavow his own pain, but a stone grew in his chest and he could no longer speak.

21

Daniel was allowed a second visit with Sarah. As soon as he entered her room, she pointed toward a paper cup that contained ice chips and a plastic spoon. Then she pointed to her mouth, so Daniel carefully placed a few ice chips on her tongue. "The ice helps me talk," Sarah said in a hoarse voice.

Daniel took her hand. "We will have plenty of time to talk later. Maybe it is best to rest your voice."

"No I have to talk now. More ice?" After sucking a few more chips, she said. "Ingrid promised she would teach me more about sailing when I'm better. Will you come?"

"There is no better person to teach you than Ingrid. And yes, of course I will come too."

"I need you to teach me how to use the compass." She looked at the bedside stand. "Let me see which way it points." He carefully set the compass on the bed so she could see it, but the card continued to rotate. "Which way is my home?"

He tried to remember the orientation of Kristiansand, and then the orientation of the hospital to the city, but he became confused. Maybe he would guess, but then he saw that

Sarah's eyes were closed. She did not respond when he gently called her name. As he returned the compass to the stand, he said in a low voice, "Oh Sarah, I do not know where anything is from here." Or from anywhere, he thought. I am just like this compass. He wiped a tear from his cheek, and then he held her hand until a nurse asked him to leave.

Ingrid decided to return to Lillesand that evening. She would call in the morning, and then decide when she should come back. Tom did not intend to leave, and Daniel decided to stay as well.

Daniel and Tom talked about their lives, and their regrets. They talked until every sentence was punctuated by a yawn. Slumped in a chair, unable to keep his head from bobbing, Daniel slid into sleep and dreamed of drifting in an open boat.

The sea, unmarked by vessel and stretching to infinity, was as still as a forest pool. Soon, Daniel discovered he could make the boat change course with his mind. In front of him, he saw Sarah's compass; sometimes its card spun in circles, and sometimes it held true. By trial, he found a direction that held the compass steady. If he deviated from that heading, by even a few degrees, the compass became erratic. He marvelled at a compass that could select a course for him. But where was the compass directing him?

Without warning, a violent storm came over the sea, and

it took all of Daniel's concentration to maintain his course. Enormous swells threatened to capsize the little boat, but the compass knew which heading would take the waves head-on. Black clouds swept across the sky and blocked the sun, so that he had to lean forward to see the instrument. With his face almost against the glass he could see the card start to spin; he tried one heading after another, but it was clear—he had lost control. He felt the boat lift and drop. The cover glass shattered. Wind tore the card away. The roar of an immense swell rushed at the boat from abeam. As the boat rolled he screamed, and the scream woke him.

Trembling and disoriented, Daniel tried to absorb the harsh fluorescent-lit reality around him. Tom was gone. Unwilling to face another dream, he stood and began to pace. A woman dashed into the lounge. "Are you with Mr. Fielding?" she asked breathlessly. "You must come at once and help."

When they turned into the corridor that led to the intensive care unit, he saw a blur of movement and a cluster of people. Then he saw Tom. He was sitting on the carpet with his back against the wall. Over and over, he brought his fists down on the floor; each time he yelled "No." Someone knelt on either side of him; a nurse motioned for Daniel to come and assist, but Daniel darted past them, and ran to Sarah's room.

Alarms wailed. Someone pressed a mask tight on Sarah's face. Another quickly transferred the monitors from a shelf to her bed. Someone kicked at the wheel locks, and in almost no time the team was heading for the door with Sarah. He understood from the exchanges that she required urgent surgery. Daniel reached for her arm, but a hand firmly pushed him away. In the shuffle, the bedside stand tumbled, and the compass fell to the floor. The cover glass shattered, and the twisting card became still at last.

The news came in the early hours—Sarah was in a coma with a slim chance of recovery. She returned to the intensive care unit, but later she would most likely spend her days in a ward. If she were lucky, maybe a rehabilitation facility in Oslo.

Daniel remembered seeing Tom cry; Ingrid came and cried too, but Daniel felt—from the moment he saw Sarah's unseeing gaze—that his spirit departed. He remained in Kristiansand for several days to assist Tom. Aside from essential communications, he avoided speaking to anyone. Nothing held his interest; he blocked the past, and the future was too abstract to warrant attention. After Tom found a room to rent near the hospital, Daniel returned to Lillesand and took a room at The Kettle where he refused to answer the phone.

After two days, someone knocked on Daniel's door, but he remained silent in the room. Later another knock, and another, and then a key turned in the lock. A woman holding a bundle of towels entered, and Daniel rose to apologize, but then he saw—close behind—Eric Haugen.

"Come Daniel, we are going to the harbour," Eric said firmly.

"It is best if I stay by myself for now."

"Do you remember last spring? After you ran your boat onto the beach, and you could not breathe?"

"Eric, you have my undying—"

"I did not come here to ask for your gratitude. I came here now to ask for a small favour. Will you come with me?"

Without explanation, Eric walked with Daniel to the harbour, took him aboard his launch, and motored far enough from the harbour so no one could see or hear what took place on deck. Then Eric cut the power to where the boat's progress was imperceptible, and set out a vacuum bottle. "First we will have coffee." After pouring coffee into a cup for Daniel, he produced a flask and dumped a generous portion of its contents into the coffee. "I understand you like coffee with character."

The coffee burned Daniel's throat, and he felt heat radiate through his body. When the cup was half empty, in spite of his protest, Eric filled it again from his flask. The combined effects of the growing warmth, the smell of the sea air, and the gentle rocking of the launch caused Daniel to accept that being with Eric was preferable to staying in his room.

"You are getting some colour back in your face," Eric said. "Now, I want you to tell me what happened at Kristiansand."

"Surely Ingrid has told you everything."

"I want to hear it from you."

"You know what happened."

"Tell me."

Unable to refuse Eric, he began his story when Ingrid first told him about Sarah. He drank more and talked more, and Eric remained quiet. When he came to where he woke from his dream and Tom was missing, he jumped to his feet and threw the rum laced coffee into the sea. "No more. You have your favour, now take me back."

"No," Eric said calmly.

"Are we to sit here all day?"

"What happened when you found Tom missing?"

In his mind, Daniel saw Tom striking the floor, and he rushed ahead to Sarah's room. He remembered her unseeing eyes, and a wave of sorrow flowed over him and engulfed him. For the first time since the hospital, he cried. And all the grief he had ever known was joined.

The sun was low in the sky, when Eric's launch entered Lillesand harbour. "It is time for a good meal and some real coffee," Eric said. "Agree with me on one thing. Neither of us will ever speak of this trip to anyone, not even to each other."

"Agreed, and thank you my friend."

Eric laughed. "Thank me for what? We have not even been together. So, you will need a place to stay. You cannot stay at The Kettle forever."

"The first thing I want to do is gather my things on the island. I can do that tomorrow by water taxi."

"This is your water taxi,"

"No I want to spend the day alone. To say goodbye. It will be the last time."

"Then I will leave you there and return when you say. I insist."

Eric left Daniel at the island at nine in the morning and promised to return at four. Daniel found his scattered belongings heaped in a pile. If a visitor made footprints, the wind-shifted soot had erased them. With a cold wind blowing, he was glad to step into his foul weather gear. He would leave his gear at the cabin site, and spend the day at the cove. The eerie quiet of the island unsettled him, and he wondered if it had always been like that, or if he had changed in some way.

It was comforting to walk the familiar trail. The cut trees at the cove saddened him but he no longer felt angry. Looking at the scene, he imagined a park-like setting. There was a bronze plaque on a prominent rock. It would be a fine memorial. Naturally, there would have to be a sign warning of the current. As the sun began to warm the cove, he pictured Emma building a sand castle in the sand. In the past, such an image would come to him with the terror of a nightmare, but at that moment, he felt comforted by that memory, and yet there was still an undertow of sorrow.

As the hours passed, Daniel felt increasingly at peace with his decision to leave forever. It would be best to leave it to the law, to the will of the community, to fate. He would stay informed, and get involved if it would help. Ingrid was right, there was plenty of work for experienced carpenters, and he could look for a place to stay. Maybe an inexpensive place that he could fix up. Lillesand was where he was born, and Lillesand was where he had friends.

There was only an hour left, so he sat on the bench and tried to burn the image of the cove into his memory. Then he looked out over the sea and said goodbye.

He heard footfalls from the trail, and assumed that Eric had come early. Without turning, he called, "Over here by the beach. Come and join me." The noise stopped, so he turned to look, but the walker was still in the brush. Perhaps Eric was confused. "Just stay on the path, you cannot miss me." Just then, Birk emerged from the trail, followed by his wife and son.

22

"What're you doing here?" Birk asked as he entered the cove. "Haven't you given me enough trouble?" He came swiftly toward Daniel, but slowed as Daniel stood and towered above him. Just beyond Daniel's reach, he stopped and thrust his head forward. "If I'd known you'd—"

"Birk, please?" Laura pleaded.

"Leave us alone," Birk said through clenched teeth.

"Will you satisfy my curiosity?" Daniel asked. "If your plan was to develop this part of the island, why did you need to remove the cabin?"

Birk's hands folded into fists. "Don't you mock me. You know damn well what happened."

"Yes I know what you did, but not why."

Laura stepped closer. "You have a lot of nerve Mr. Nordal. To accuse my husband after what happened." Her body shook with anger.

What Daniel heard, he could not fathom. Why were they so angry? The shed? There was nothing to do, but to take responsibility. After taking a deep breath, he concentrated on speaking slow and calm. "When I saw what you did to the cabin, I became unreasonable, and I did the same to your tool shed. I will pay for the loss. As for the cabin, I would like to know why."

"You don't know do you?" Laura asked. "The fire marshal declared the cabin was destroyed by a lightning strike. We wanted to keep the cabin."

"I play the fool again it seems. I will pay as I said." Daniel saw that Robert was climbing on a limb over the water. "Your son—"

"That boy is none of your business," Birk said. "And who the hell is that Jacobsen woman you sent to my stepmother?"

"Solveig talked with Anna?"

"Let's go," Laura said. "There's no point to this, and it's getting cold."

"No we stay," Birk said. "I chartered that boat for the day."

"What happened between Solveig and Anna?" Daniel asked.

Laura looked intently at Daniel. "You really don't know?"

"This is the first—"

"You didn't ask Solveig Jacobsen to talk with Birk's stepmother?"

Daniel shook his head.

Birk took Robert on his shoulders, and strolled along the shore. The boy started to scream. "Put me down." He squirmed loose from Birk's shoulders; Birk had to set him down, and he ran in circles with Birk giving chase. At last, Birk caught Robert by his arm, and they both tumbled to the ground.

"Just sit with him for a minute," Laura said. "This has been too much for him." Under her breath, she added, "Too much for all of us." She turned her attention to Daniel. "Birk decided that a development here was too much trouble and cost too much." She turned her head. "Watch him—he's wandering off." She moaned under her breath. "We decided to upgrade the cabin and use it for family vacations. When we learned about the fire, Birk called his stepmother to tell her and discovered that she had changed her mind." Laura shook her head. "She gave the island to the county." She looked around and shrugged "So, we came today for a last look."

Daniel watched Laura pick up her son, and for the first time he felt compassion for the family. The boy calmed, and Laura sat on the ground with him next to Birk. It seems we all have come for a last look, Daniel thought. Laura would have no reason to lie. It seems it is all over. "I think it is best if I leave you all alone," Daniel said. "I have arranged for a boat." He looked at his watch. "It will be another hour, but I will disappear until then."

Birk began to shout. "What an act. Maybe you can con my stepmother and everyone else, but you can't con me. You're obsessed with living alone here. You're a lunatic. No one else can have this island, if you can't. That's it." He stood and pushed his face close to Daniel. "Isn't that right?"

Seeing the terror in the boy's eyes, Daniel turned and stepped away. The stress of the encounter was causing his lungs to tighten, and he had left his inhaler with his change of clothes at the cabin site. It would be best to leave now. Turning his head he saw Birk, he saw pain, he saw fear, and he saw himself.

Then he turned and saw Robert; the boy had climbed out over the water again. The limb dipped, and he heard the sharp report of cracking timber. He shouted and forced his body to run.

The boy fell and Laura screamed. Birk was close on Daniel's heels so that when Daniel slowed at the water's edge, Birk smashed into his back and they both fell into the sea.

As Daniel's face struck the cold surface, he gasped and inhaled water, and as he rolled to bring his face above water, paroxysms of cough racked his body. Birk grabbed Robert, and Daniel could see from the thrashing that Birk did not have a foothold. The boy and his father were between Daniel and the shore, so Daniel brought his knees up, and pushed against Birk to drive them toward shore. Birk was able to climb out with Robert in his arms. He looked fleetingly at Daniel, but Daniel motioned for him to leave.

Daniel tried to speak, but he coughed with each word. "Go warm the boy." He gasped. "Blanket at the cabin site." He could not say more, so he pointed to the trail with one hand and paddled with the other. Laura started to approach but he waved her away. Soon, he was alone.

Running and coughing had put a strangle hold on his already tight lungs, and in the effort to push Birk to shore, he had propelled himself into deeper water. There was some buoyancy from the air trapped in his foul weather gear, but from the stream of bubbles around him, he knew the gear would soon drag him under unless he came ashore at once. Though a strong swimmer, with his lungs bound by spasm, it was all he could do to tread water against the current. Knowing that fighting the current would kill him, he rolled on his back and tried to float, but the frigid water rapidly infiltrated his gear; he started to shiver.

It became clear. He would die. Either the cold would do it or he would drown. Does it matter? Either way he would be unconscious soon; that would be merciful. There could be no more fitting place than this to end his life. Would he see Linda and Emma? It became difficult to hold a thought or an image. Icy water lapped at his ears. Time disappeared, and he ceased to examine his condition.

An intense throbbing penetrated to his mind. Can you hear your heart as it fails? Something slammed into his side, and his collar seemed to be lifting him as his back slid along a hard surface.

"If I can hold you here with a hook in your jacket, maybe I can get a rope under your arms." Eric said.

You are too late my friend. You should not have to witness my death. A deep sense of comfort replaced the numbing cold. A part of his brain understood, he had heard of this before; the end was here. More than anything, he wanted to sleep. Then Eric's boat shook and rolled, and there were other voices. His body rose, and just before he passed into sleep, he heard fragments of speech. "Radio . . . landing space . . . barely breathing."

Hands disturbed him. Movement—radio chatter—a decision is made—go to Arendal. Many hands crawling like mice. One arm wrapped, the other punctured. Pressure on his face, and scissors snipping. A force, cold and wet pressed on his chest, and then blessed sleep.

Something new! A tube rose from his mouth, and joined with a bag that someone squeezed. Each squeeze sounded like a fart. With whom could he share this joke? Suddenly the world moved, and he came to stare at a close metal ceiling. The world shook and roared.

"Squeeze your right hand," the fart-maker commanded. He obeyed. "Squeeze your left hand." He obeyed again. "Do not bite on the tube."

He tried to argue the point, but no sound came. Someone said "respiratory arrest." Would he have to go to jail now? Another joke he could not share.

Deciding that the tube in his mouth kept him from speaking, he reached to remove the offending device. Immediately, two jumpsuited jailors strapped his arms. One of them tinkered with a tube in Daniel's arm, and consciousness faded once again.

Daniel remained on life support for two days, and for two days, he remained unaware. At last, he came face to face with the wonder that he lived, and the wonder that he still had choices to make. With the voice-stealing tube removed, he transferred to a quiet room.

The first visitor that Daniel was aware of was Eric, to whom he repeatedly expressed his gratitude. After Eric silenced him, and inquired about his health, Daniel pressed for information about Robert.

"As I approached the island to pick you up, I saw another launch. The first person I recognized was Birk. He was coming down from the bluff looking like a drowned rat. My first thought was; you gave him a dunking. Then his wife came along with their child wrapped in a blanket. By the time I came alongside everyone was on board so I hailed Knut, the skipper Birk hired, and asked if I could help. He said there might still be someone in the water on the leeward side of the island, so I wasted no time." Eric shrugged. "That is all there is."

"You saw Robert?"

Eric smiled. "You almost died, and you worry about the boy. Well Daniel, Knut the skipper I told you about, has a heated cabin on his launch so I imagine the lad got to dry off, and after we tended to you, he took his passengers to the clinic—just to be safe. Birk had chills, but everyone checked out okay.

Daniel shook his head. "Was it Knut I heard with you?"

"Yes, thank God. He followed right behind me to the cove. If not for him, well I am not sure. He had a radio, which saved your life. A rescue boat came, and took you to an island where a helicopter could land."

"Did the Olsens witness this?"

"Certainly, they were on Knut's boat."

"They should not have to witness such things." He sighed. "What a strange thing Eric; all I wanted to do was to have a quiet day. To say goodbye."

"Did you get to do that?"

Daniel laughed. "Oh yes, not only did I get to say goodbye, but I almost said hello."

"It is good that you can joke about it. Now what can I do for you?"

"You have done too much, but there is one small thing. Real coffee," he said in a whisper.

Eric chuckled. "It is time they kicked you out of here. Smuggling coffee should be an easy task."

Ingrid stood at the open door with a package in her hand and knocked. "I see you have a visitor; I can come back later."

Eric jumped up and took Ingrid by the arm. "Nonsense! I

was just leaving." He turned to Daniel and winked, "It could take a long time to find just the right coffee."

She took his hand in both of hers, leaned over, and kissed him on the cheek. "Daniel Nordal, what on earth have you gotten into now?"

"No more Ingrid. No more." He cleared his throat. "First, is there any change with Sarah?" Daniel watched Ingrid slowly shake her head. "And Tom, how is he holding up?'

"Solveig has come to stay with him in Kristiansand."

"Good, he should not be alone at a time like this."

"But what about you Daniel?"

"By some great mystery I am still here. What matters now is what happens to Sarah, and Tom. No, what happens to all of us, even Birk. I hope he finds peace."

Ingrid pulled her braid forward, and began to unravel it.

"What is on your mind?" Daniel asked.

"Oh!" She let the braid drop. "I have to stop doing that; it always gives me away." She picked up the parcel she brought and held it out to him. "Would you take a look at this?"

Fumbling with the package, he managed to tear it open. Inside was the compass he had given to Sarah. The glass was missing, and the card was loose in the box.

"Tom is certain that Sarah will recover," Ingrid said, "and she will want to see her compass. He is worried how she will react to the damage. I said I would see what I could do, but I do not know what to do Daniel."

"I think a good instrument maker or the company that built it could put it right. If not, I would be very happy to buy a replacement compass for the case. The main thing for Tom, for all of us, is hope. This piece of metal is a small thing. I hope with all my heart for Sarah's recovery."

Ingrid took Daniel's hand and held tight. "All of these changes Daniel, it must be so hard for you. Now you have no home. Would you like to sleep on the sloop until you get settled?"

Was he homeless now? As he pondered the question, he realized that he had been homeless for a long time. And he remembered, the day he lit fire to the shed, sensing the words from Linda, *go home Daniel.* Or did the words come from his soul?

There was a night, he remembered; he was lying in the dark while Ingrid slept. He remembered looking at the stars through the port, while he listened to and felt Ingrid breathe. He remembered the weight of her head on his chest and the wetness of his skin by her mouth. It was a time when all of his being, all of his past and all of his future, converged into a single-minded focus. He remembered that he felt at home.

"Yes Ingrid, I would like that. Maybe for a day or two until I can get my bearings."

The author wishes to thank the following for their contributions: Pål Brekke for an eyewitness account of medical evacuation at Lyngør; Bjørn Skeie MD PhD for medical evacuation procedures in Lillesand area; Erland Dyrstad, Harbour Master, Lillesand, for specific sailing times along the coast.

Lightning Source UK Ltd.
Milton Keynes UK
UKOW052131180712

196238UK00003B/13/P